DATE DUE

AUG 2 1 2015

PRINTED IN U.S.A.

7 BILLION LIVES ARE IN DANGER.
13 STRANGERS WITH TERRIFYING NIGHTMARES.
1 ENEMY WILL STOP AT NOTHING TO DESTROY US ALL.

MY NAME IS SAM.
I AM ONE OF THE LAST THIRTEEN.
OUR BATTLE BEGINS HERE.

THE LAST
THIRTEEN

BOOK ONE

ARE YOU ONE OF THEM?

ACADEMY School for teaching gifted students to true dream. Professor Tom McPherson follows a long history of Academy mantra whereby true Dreamers use wisdom, studies from history and obtainment of knowledge to have powerful influence across the world. Ruled by the Dreamer Council.

ENTERPRISE Organization committed to economic gain. Undertakes scientific research and genetic testing to uncover the cause of true dreaming. Director Jack Palmer battles with his own Agents, who see true Dreamers as potential weapons.

ENEMY A nightmare creature come to life. Solaris has haunted true Dreamers' nightmares for centuries, and manifests for the final battle to rule the world. An armored, shadowy figure, who unleashes destruction upon anything that stands in the way of ultimate power. The thing the last 13 must stop, or it will destroy us all.

This one's for my friend Emily McDonald—JP.

First American Edition 2013
Kane Miller, A Division of EDC Publishing

Text copyright © James Phelan, 2013.
Cover design © Scholastic Australia, 2013.
Illustrations by Chad Mitchell.
Design by Nicole Stofberg.

First published by Scholastic Australia Pty Limited in 2013
This edition published under license from Scholastic Australia Pty Limited.

Cover photography: Manhattan © istockphoto.com/Pawel Gaul; Statue Of Liberty © istockphoto.com/
Katrin Solansky; Blueprint © istockphoto.com/Adam Korzekwa; Parkour tic-tac © istockphoto.com/Willie
B. Thomas; Climbing wall © istockphoto.com/microgen; Leonardo da Vinci (Sepia) © istockphoto.com/
pictore; NY sunset © istockphoto.com/Adam Kazmierski; Gears © istockphoto.com/-Oxford-; Mechanical
blueprint © istockphoto.com/teekid; Circuit board © istockphoto.com/Bjorn Meyer; Map © istockphoto.com/
alengo; Grunge drawing © istockphoto.com/aleksandar velasevic; World map © istockphoto.com/Maksim
Pasko; internet © istockphoto.com/Andrey Prokhorov; Inside clock © istockphoto.com/LdF; Space galaxy ©
istockphoto.com/Sergii Tsololo; Sunset © istockphoto.com/Joakim Leroy; Manhattan2 © istockphoto.com/
Nikki Bidgood; Blue flare © istockphoto.com/YouraPechkin; Global communication © istockphoto.com/chadive
samanthakamani; Brooklyn bridge © istockphoto.com/franckreporter; Earth satellites © istockphoto.com/
Alexey Popov; Girl portrait © istockphoto.com/peter zelei; Student & board © istockphoto.com/zhang bo;
Young man serious © istockphoto.com/Jacob Wackerhausen; Portrait man © istockphoto.com/Alina Solovyova-
Vincent; Sad expression © istockphoto.com/Shelly Perry; Content man © istockphoto.com/drbimages; Pensive
man © istockphoto.com/Chuck Schmidt; Black and pink © istockphoto.com/blackwaterimages; Punk girl ©
istockphoto.com/Kuzma; Aerial city © Jupiterimages/Photos.com; Woman escaping © Jose antonio Sanchez
reyes/Photos.com; Young running man © Tatiana Belova/Photos.com; Gears clock © Jupiterimages/Photos.com;
Young woman © Anomen/Photos.com ; NY, NY © Pontus Edenberg/Photos.com; Sunset NY © Pål Sundsøy
| Dreamstime.com; Explosions © Leigh Prather | Dreamstime.com; Jump over wall © Ammentorp |
Dreamstime.com; Mountains, CAN © Akadiusz Iwanicki | Dreamstime.com; Sphinx Bucegi © Adrian Nicolae |
Dreamstime.com; Big mountains © Hoptrop | Dreamstime.com; Sunset mountains © Pklimenko | Dreamstime.
com; Mountains lake © Janmika | Dreamstime.com; Blue night sky © Mack2happy | Dreamstime.com; Old
writing © Empire331 | Dreamstime.com; Young man © Shuen Ho Wang | Dreamstime.com; Abstract cells ©
Sur | Dreamstime.com; Helicopter © Evren Kalinbacak | Dreamstime.com; Aeroplane © Rgbe | Dreamstime.
com; Phrenology illustration © Mcarrel | Dreamstime.com; Abstract interior © Sur | Dreamstime.com; Papyrus
© Cebreros | Dreamstime.com; Blue shades © Mohamed Osama | Dreamstime.com; Blue background ©
Matusciac | Dreamstime.com; Sphinx and Pyramid © Dan Breckwoldt | Dreamstime.com; Blue background2
© Cammeraydave | Dreamstime.com; Abstract shapes © Lisa Mckown | Dreamstime.com; Yellow Field ©
Simon Greig | Dreamstime.com; Blue background3 © Sergey Skrebnev | Dreamstime.com; Blue eye © Richard
Thomas | Dreamstime.com; Abstract landscape © Crazy80frog | Dreamstime.com; Rameses II © Jose I. Soto
| Dreamstime.com; Helicopter © Sculpies | Dreamstime.com; Vitruvian man © Cornelius20 | Dreamstime.
com; Scarab beetle © Charon | Dreamstime.com; Eye of Horus © Charon | Dreamstime.com; Handsome male
portrait © DigitalHand Studio/Shutterstock.com; Teen girl © CREATISTA/Shutterstock.com.

For information contact:
Kane Miller, A Division of EDC Publishing
PO Box 470663
Tulsa, OK 74147-0663
www.kanemiller.com
www.edcpub.com
www.usbornebooksandmore.com

Library of Congress Control Number: 2013942845

Printed and bound in the United States of America
2 3 4 5 6 7 8 9 10
ISBN: 978-1-61067-254-2

THE LAST
THIRTEEN

BOOK ONE

JAMES PHELAN

Kane Miller
A DIVISION OF EDC PUBLISHING

BREAKING NEWS

In recent weeks, a group has emerged with what can perhaps be described as a special "gift" or "ability": their dreams come true.

Although unaware of it now, these individuals will not only save the world, but change it forever. They are our last hope in a battle of good versus evil.

This transformation from ordinary to extraordinary, this journey, will not occur overnight. Every story has a beginning.

"I click my fingers," the deep, scratchy voice says, "and everyone around us dies." I struggle to focus on the dark, imposing figure before me. Behind, there's a crater of shattered pavement, as though it has crashed down to earth from the sky. Concrete dust coats its black full-body armor which shimmers slightly as though in a heat haze. The face is completely masked. Even the eyes and mouth are hidden behind wire mesh, the only chinks in the sleek metal facade. The whole being vibrates like it's not completely solid. A shiver runs down my spine.

Is this what death looks like?

I instinctively turn towards my redheaded companion, Lora. At first, I think she's frozen like the rest of the world around us. While birds have paused mid-flight and a torn-out page of a discarded newspaper is suspended in the still air, she has remained motionless, facing away from this hideous apparition. But then I realize, *she cannot see it*.

"Ah, I see . . . *especially* her," the figure says, seeing my gaze flicker to Lora. It moves closer, now only ten paces away, and the mask glints reflectively as it catches the sun's rays. The monster looks as if it's been drawn with sharp, scratchy pen, like moving lines of black ink tattooed viciously on to a human shape. The sight of this being makes my eyes hurt and my head scream with its repulsiveness.

"This is between us," I say through gritted teeth.

Lora looks around. Her green eyes penetrating, but yet unseeing. "Who are you talking to?" she asks.

"Stay where you are, Lora, just keep looking the other way," I caution her, my instinct telling me to keep her away, keep her safe, even though she is much older than me.

"Ah, yes, the great Sam, finder of the last 13, the supposed *hero* who shows others the way."

What is this thing, and what kind of hero does it think I am?

"So brave, right until the end . . ." Its voice rattles around inside my skull. "At the final battle, just like the prophecy says, you will lead me to my rightful power, thinking all the while that you are saving these foolish people."

"Prophecy?"

"Enough! You know why I'm here, boy . . . hand it over."

I have no idea what it is talking about but then I sense a weight in my pocket. I have something important that this thing wants . . . this heavy, round object. So now I know why it is here.

"I have what you want."

"Yes, you *do* . . . where is it?"

I reach into my pocket and retrieve a dark crystal sphere.

"Yes, that's it . . ." The blurred figure seems to shimmer at a higher frequency as though excited. "Give it to me."

"And then?"

"Then . . . then I *might* let your friend live."

"And everyone else?"

The figure shrugs and every movement of its form leaves a slight disturbance in the air around it, a smoky haze. It's as though I can sense a grisly smile behind the mask.

"One *click* of my fingers," its voice quiets, becoming even more ominous, "and everything around us *burns*. Think about that, golden boy. Everyone. Gone."

Black-gloved hands mime clicking fingers and I shudder.

"Good . . . you're scared. Now, hand the crystal over." It steps closer. "Give it to me and your friend will be spared."

I open my hand.

"Yes, that's it, hand it to me," the black figure commands.

I hold it out with a tenuous grip, as if it may fall at any second.

"What are you doing?" it says, the amplified voice more urgent.

"You'll kill us all anyway."

"No!" The tall figure takes a stride towards me. "Don't be a fool!"

"I will if you don't promise−"

It steps towards me again and I toss the crystal up into the air.

The figure moves in a blur, diving forward, reaching out

for the falling sphere.

I lunge towards Lora, pulling her to me.

"Sam, what did you—"

"Get down!" I yell as we hit the ground.

The figure grasps the crystal. As it does, it raises its other hand.

I am too late.

Fire radiates out.

Everything around us—people, cars, buildings—glows from within and then explodes in quick succession.

Ash and debris fill the air as Lora begins to glow and grows warm in my embrace. I close my eyes and before she has a chance to flash brightly, both she and I are—

Gone.

"**N**O!" Sam yelled. He sat bolt upright in bed, bathed in a cold sweat, his heart hammering in his chest.

"Today in Vancouver, a mostly warm, sunny day . . ." the radio DJ announced.

Vancouver. I can't believe it's been a year since we moved here.

Sam looked at the alarm clock—7:43 a.m. His eyes automatically went to the black notebook next to the clock. He knew he should fill it in, follow this little ritual his dream-specialist psychiatrist had been making him do all year to help improve his sleep, to keep the nightmares away. By writing it down, he was meant to relive all the horrifying details blow by blow, just so they could "explore" it in their sessions. *Yeah, it's working great . . .*

With a sigh, Sam picked up the book and started scribbling down what he remembered from the nightmare. A friend called Lora—she had red hair, green eyes. Looked about twenty-five. His handwriting was shaky but he concentrated and pressed hard, steadying his hand and recording what he could. As he recalled the rest of the nightmare he felt details already slipping away, becoming lost to the waking world, so he wrote in a scribbled frenzy. He finished by writing, "the last 13," then underlining and circling it for emphasis . . . *the last thirteen what?*

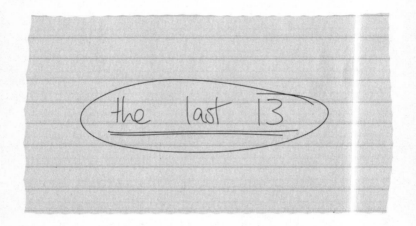

Sam sat on the edge of his bed, resting his forehead on his hands, elbows on his knees, scrunching the lush carpet between his toes. His messy brown hair was wet with sweat and his heart was still racing as though he'd been running. He closed his eyes and took some deep breaths, settling himself. But the wrongness of the nightmare was almost tangible, and he knew it would keep him on edge all day.

The bedroom door opened. Sam's dad, Mike, stood in the doorway. "Come on, Sam, you're going to be late."

"Yeah, I know, I'll hustle," Sam replied.

"Your mother has made breakfast. I can drive you to the bus stop, but you've got to hurry."

Sam nodded.

His dad turned to leave but Sam saw him hesitate. Scout, the family beagle, ran into the room and licked at Sam's clammy toes.

"You all right?" Mike asked.

Sam looked up at him bleary-eyed. "Yeah, I'm—I'm fine. Be out in a sec."

Mike watched Sam scratching Scout's head, then looked over to the notebook.

"Bad dream again?"

Sam nodded.

"You made your notes?"

Sam nodded. His dad looked at the book like he was contemplating reading it, but then let it be.

"Well, all right then, get ready for school—we don't need your mom going all supernova on us."

Sam smiled. "OK, Dad."

But his dad just stood there, watching him. "You want me to cancel your jujitsu class tonight?"

"Nah, I'll be fine. In fact, it'll be great to go and kick some butt!"

Mike nodded and left, his heavy footsteps fading away.

Scout's dopey face stared up at Sam, so friendly, always inquisitive, always understanding in some inexplicable way. Sam tried to remember more of his nightmare but couldn't, it had already faded to next to nothing. The psychiatrist his parents had sent him to, Dr. Dark, said it would get easier, that he'd condition himself to remember and write episodes down verbatim. *That hasn't really worked out yet* . . . Through analyzing the notes, Sam could supposedly learn to control where his dreams took him. Somehow through *that*, he'd have fewer nightmares. *Yeah, right.* Three months later, and still the terrors woke him every other night, still he didn't remember anything but a few small details, like running away . . . from someone, or from something *on fire*. It was always the fire that woke him.

Sam walked into the bathroom, had a shower and got out before the egg timer on the soap dish went off. His mother, Jane's, latest project was saving water. *Maybe a longer shower would calm me down, give me fewer nightmares—thought of that, Mom?* In the mirror, Sam looked for changes, but he was still average height, average build, brown eyes and brown hair. Mr. Average. The scar from the accident was still there, but Sam was hoping for rippling abs and pumped guns. He'd been playing all kinds of sports to help tire him out and sleep better . . . but there was nothing to show for it. *Maybe when I turn sixteen.*

"Maybe when you get bitten by a radioactive spider," Sam said to his reflection and he smiled. In his room, he threw on a fresh school shirt and yesterday's pants.

"Sam, this is your last chance!" His mom's voice cut through the house, a knife in and out of his skull. "Breakfaaast!"

Sam sat at the kitchen table. His two-year-old brother, Ben, was next to him, alternating between sculpting a mountain out of his scrambled eggs and pushing baked beans up his nose.

"Thanks for breakfast, Mom," Sam said. He poured a glass of juice but he was not paying attention, momentarily lost in a daydream, and he let the liquid overflow.

"Sam! Not again!" his mother grizzled as he quickly mopped it up. Bits and pieces of the nightmare were trickling through his mind, distracting him.

The fire alarm went off, making Sam jump from the table.

His mom ran over to the gas stove and pulled off the kitchen towel that had caught fire, dousing it in the sink with water.

"It's OK, son," Mike said, and Sam sat down, nodding.

Sam's parents sat opposite him, watching, as if waiting for him to fess up, to explain *something*, either about his problem with fire or his latest nightmare.

"Sam, are you OK?" his mother asked as he moved his food around aimlessly on the plate. Sam remained silent, lost in a vague memory of his dream.

"Sam?" his dad said, his voice soft.

"Yeah?" Sam snapped out of it, looked up.

"Is something wrong?" his mom asked. "I'm sorry about the towel just now. But you're not eating your breakfast, which is a first. It's like you're not really here."

"I—I'm OK. Just tired. I had another nightmare . . . or something."

"A nightmare?" His parents remained expectant, gently prodding him to continue. "About what? The fire again?"

"No, not exactly. It was about . . . I honestly don't know." Sam drank his juice. "I can only remember bits of it . . ."

Sam's dad put his newspaper down, sipped his coffee, and looked from his wife to Sam.

"You want to tell us about it?" his dad offered. "Take your time. If you miss your bus I can drop you off later . . . maybe we can even book you in to see Dr.—"

"No, it's OK, thanks." Sam hurriedly shook his head, and with great concentration ate a forkful of scrambled eggs.

His mother asked, "Was it a new dream last night?"

Sam nodded.

"Did you write it down?"

"Yeah . . . some—I mean—I tried."

Sam's parents glanced at each other. Ben threw a piece of toast. Sam ducked and it bounced off the wall and onto the floor where Scout vacuumed it up without chewing.

"Sam," his mom said, "you know you need to write it all down."

"I really tried—"

"You'll forget the details otherwise."

"I want to forget them!" Sam pushed his plate away. His parents were silent. "I want to forget all of it. I want to forget what happened to Bill . . ."

Sam's parents' worried look was enough to make him realize he had scared them. No way was he getting out of a visit to Dr. Dark now. The fire that had killed his best friend last year was the reason he'd started seeing the psychiatrist in the first place, and Sam knew he'd have to work hard to make his parents understand that this dream was something new. "It was a really horrible nightmare, OK? Worse this time. It wasn't about the fire. But it was so vivid. Everything around me—people were getting killed by this . . . this *thing*. This *evil* thing."

"Thing?"

"Well, yeah. I mean, I think it was a man. It was a tall dark figure in some kind of special suit, all black, fully masked . . . kind of looked like he was shimmering."

"Go on . . ."

"He was able to—he shot *fire* out of his *hand*, and . . ." Sam said, feeling a little stupid saying it aloud and all too aware of the concern mentioning *fire* again would raise. "And I think he was able to freeze everything: the cars, all the people, time itself . . ."

Sam strained to think back, to recall it.

"Everyone was frozen and this figure wanted . . . I

can't remember, exactly, something about a prophecy, a crystal ball, and something about a final 13? The last thing I remember was him clicking his fingers and everything caught fire. There was this big flash and it was hot and bright. Then I woke up, screaming. Is that enough detail for you?"

His parents shared a concerned look, then his father looked away and his mother looked straight at him.

"You know we're only trying to help you," his mother said. "You need to accept that Bill's death wasn't your fault. There was no way you or anyone could have saved him. It's a miracle you got out when you did. This new nightmare could just be you finding another way to punish yourself. But we can help you get better, if, as Dr. Dark says, you can train yourself to remember—"

Sam stood up angrily and headed for his bedroom, but then stopped by the kitchen door, turned around and said quietly, "It wasn't about that. This thing, this evil guy, he was going to kill them all, I remember that. No matter what I did, he was always going to kill them."

"Who was it?" his dad asked.

"I don't know, but he sure knew me."

"Sam," his mom said, "what exactly did he look like?"

"I told you, he wore a mask . . ." Sam said, slowly forcing himself to recall more specific details. "He wore a black mask, which even covered his eyes, and a black bodysuit. It was in a constant state of movement, like it was a heat mirage. And I could tell, through his voice and his motions, that he was *enjoying* himself, being in control like that . . . and then everyone died. He burned them all."

"Dressed all in black . . ." his dad said thoughtfully. "And his voice . . . "

"His voice was weird," Sam said, remembering the tone and volume of it. "Like it was amplified and scrambled or something. Metallic. Disguised."

"OK," his dad said. "Go get your things. I'll drive you to school, and we'll make you an appointment with Dr. Dark for this afternoon."

Sam went to get ready. His parents seemed to be taking him seriously, which made it even harder to shake off the feeling that something was now suddenly wrong in the world. Very wrong.

Two hours later, Sam was sitting in his high school classroom. The room was quiet as the science teacher, Mr. Cole, waited for the students to finish a surprise test. Sam couldn't concentrate, as parts of his nightmare kept popping into his head, along with his parents' incessant questions about his dreams. Absentmindedly filling in the answers, it seemed like in no time the test papers were being passed forward to the teacher's desk.

"So, that wraps up Einstein," Mr. Cole said. Mr. Cole was OK. Sam had attended the school since the start of last year, and coincidentally, so had Mr. Cole. The coincidence being that Mr. Cole had taught at his old high school back in Toronto, where he had been a teacher of his for some class or other, pretty much every year. He looked like he was about his parents' age, and had glasses and a beard which made him seem quite friendly and relaxed, almost cool . . . *until you see those ties*, Sam thought. Today's shocker read: "It's sedimentary, my dear Watson." It was even more awful than his dad's jokes.

Mr. Cole constantly pushed Sam, harder than any other

student it seemed, always expecting him to get the top grade. Sam felt strangely compelled to make him proud and always tried his best. He might not top the class each time, but he did well.

"This week, as you know, we're recapping physics, to prepare for your final exams," Mr. Cole said.

Groans chorused from the other students in the class. *It could be worse*, Sam thought, *Mr. Cole could have asked me to . . .*

"Sam, refresh our memories," Mr. Cole said. "What can you tell us about Newton's laws of motion?"

"Um—"

"Um?" Mr. Cole interjected. "As in, the unit symbol for micrometer?"

"No, sir," Sam said, "I mean, I'm sorry, I don't feel . . . Newton said that for every action, there is an equal and opposite reaction."

"That's a good answer, if I was only asking about the third law," Mr. Cole said. "What about the first and second?"

Sam bit his lip and thought about it. He knew it was something about motion being uniform unless changed by an object.

Xavier answered. He was the brains of the class, yet somehow the popular kid too. It was probably because he came from one of the richest families in the country. Money, brains, *and* he was good at sports. It was a lethal combo it seemed for the girls of the school, for with his dark hair and blue eyes, he seemed to get all the attention, all the time. Sam had been a little wary of him since day one because Xavier's father was Dr. Dark, the renowned psychiatrist, and Sam's dream analyst. Xavier was droning on, explaining Newton's laws by relating them to his family's private jet in flight. *Loser.* Sam had been right about the motion thing, though.

"Great example," Mr. Cole said, drawing a diagram on the board. "So, as you can see, the applications of these laws to aerodynamics are . . ."

Sam tuned out as he looked out the window. The sun shone brightly upon the dewy grass. He blinked and got a start—a brilliant flash of light right behind his eyelids made him shift abruptly in his seat, causing his desk-mate Edward to shift away from him.

"Weirdo," Edward whispered out of the side of his mouth.

Sam ignored him, blinked again—but the vision was no longer there. *Geez,* he thought, *what's with me today?* He glanced absently out the window, trying to clear his mind—but then he saw it again, that masked face from his nightmare. Then, memories of the dream flooded back. Little flashes in quick succession, like a fast-moving slide show—his friend Lora, time frozen, the shadowy figure standing over him . . . the mask, those eyes, that voice. Saying . . . *what?*

"Sam!"

He snapped back to reality and looked around. The whole class was looking at him. The blackboard was filled from top to bottom with notes and diagrams. *Oh great, I must have been daydreaming for a while . . .*

"Sam, are you with us again?" Mr. Cole asked.

The class sniggered all around Sam.

"Yes, sir." Sam sat up straight, his face red—a mix of self-consciousness and anger.

"Well then, why don't you come up to the board and give me your answer?" Mr. Cole said, holding out the chalk. Sam scraped his chair back and walked to the front of the room, dodging a couple of out-thrust legs intent on tripping him. At the board, there was a series of different handwriting and equations—quite a few students had obviously already had their turns.

Before him:

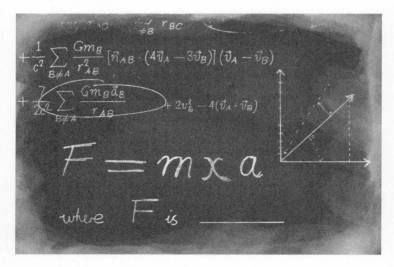

She looked from Sam to Alex.

"Maybe, a little," she said.

"Told you," Alex said, "she's a freak."

"You're a freak!" she replied.

"Yeah?" Alex said. "Well, I'm not the one who predicted all of this, am I?"

Sam looked warily between them.

"Predicted?" he said. "How?"

"She was already in here when they loaded me on board," Alex explained, nodding over to the armed soldiers. "Soon as I got on, I went to talk to her and she already knew my name! Said she knew where we were going, and how they'd soon bring on a guy named Sam from your school."

"Then—then you're with them," Sam said to her, "these soldiers?"

"No," she replied. "It's nothing like that. My name's Eva Kennedy and I was pulled out of high school, just like you guys."

"Then how did you know our names?" Sam asked. She looked down at the steel floor at her feet. "How does that work?"

Sam could see her wrists were tied just as theirs were, so it made no sense that she'd be with those guys. But he didn't know if he could trust her. *Maybe she's faking.* He noticed a tear fall from her eye to her lap, and she looked up at Sam with wet eyelashes.

"Because, Sam, I *dreamed* this," Eva said. "Last night. All of it. Beat for beat. Him. You. Them. The helicopters. All of it."

Sam felt like he was going to be sick. The fear on her face was genuine. *She dreamed all this last night—and it's coming true? But, does that mean my dream from last night could . . ?*

"I dreamed this would happen," Eva said. "That the three of us would sit here, that we would talk like this, until—"

She checked her watch.

"—about now."

Sam looked at Alex, who shrugged his shoulders and kept working away on wearing through his wrist-ties.

"That's all she told me too," he said.

"What else did you dream?" Sam asked. "Where do they take us?"

Eva bit at her bottom lip.

"What is it?"

"They don't take us anywhere," she said, as the helicopter banked hard.

Sam could see the other choppers—one out in front, the other to the side, their rotors beating fast against the air. He looked at the pilots, then imagined the three of them breaking free of their bonds and trying to overpower one or two of the soldiers, getting their weapons, forcing them to land and making a run for it . . .

"Wait," Sam said to her. "What do you mean they don't take us anywhere?"

"Yeah," Alex said. "That doesn't make any sense. We've got to be going someplace."

Eva checked her watch again.

Sam felt a heavy weight of dread in his stomach, the nausea back in full force.

"Eva, what happens?" he asked.

Eva looked at him and with a steady voice she said, "You should hang on to something."

The way she said it, the way she herself now held on to the bench seat and braced, made Sam grab hold of the bench and lean back, his legs pressing hard against the floor.

"Got it!" Alex said, revealing that he'd managed to wear through his plastic wrist-ties. He looked up to find Sam and Eva staring back at him. "What?"

"You need to hang on to something," Sam said.

"What for?"

"That," Eva said, motioning out the side window behind them. Alex and Sam craned around to see.

"Incoming, port side!" the copilot screamed into the cabin. "Brace, brace, brace!"

Behind them, a ball of fire streaming a plume of white smoke was streaking towards the helicopter—in a second they could make out a slender gray object, a missile, a supersonic bringer of death looming in on them, *fast*. They had just seconds until impact. The pilot dipped sharply towards the earth. It was an emergency dive that twisted into a sideways tilt, hurtling towards a suburban street full of life. Sam's harness gave out and he found himself crushed next to Eva, the helicopter almost completely on its side as it banked hard and fast towards the ground in the evasive maneuver.

Sam could see that Eva, while looking ill from the aircraft plummeting, didn't seem scared.

"How are you so calm right now?" Sam asked, straining to see if the missile was still closing in. *Oh boy—it's there, coming in too fast to outrun.*

"Don't worry, Sam," Eva said, her voice almost serene. "We don't die."

"How can you be so sure?" Sam asked, struggling to speak as the helicopter banked and turned haphazardly.

"Because," Eva grimaced, "I've seen what happens next."

The sound of the explosion rang in Sam's ears. The blast sucked the air from the cabin and the helicopter's tail sheared completely off, leaving a gaping hole at the rear of the aircraft. *That can't be good.* The helicopter fell fast in a flat spin towards the ground. An incessant alarm wailed. Sam was being pressed against the cabin wall, the g-forces gluing him against it like a carnival ride he'd once been on, where it had spun around so fast there was nothing he could do to get himself off the wall.

"Hang on to something!" Eva screamed.

The helicopter's nose dipped forward and that motion changed the forces inside the cabin. Alex's shoulder straps snapped free from the wall and he fell towards Sam and Eva. Sam grabbed hold of him and held tight to them both as best he could with his bound hands. He stuck his leg through some webbing straps at the back of Eva's bench seat to stop himself from being flung around.

Up front, the suited guy and a door gunner were slumped in their seats, unconscious—maybe from the blast or flying shrapnel. The frantic pilots seemed useless against the bleeping and screeching as the aircraft spun its way to earth.

Alex was screaming in Sam's ear and there was a ripping noise as the other side of the helicopter began to tear away. As the wall tore through, Alex was pulled from Sam's grasp. The only thing keeping him in the aircraft were his ankles, still strapped to the bench seat.

"Argh!" Alex screamed as his ankle straps snapped free.

Sam let go of Eva and flung his arms out to grab Alex's wrists, but right away he could feel his grip loosening as the centrifugal force threatened to throw them both out of the hole.

"Hold on!" Sam shouted over the roar of the rushing air.

"I'm trying!" Alex looked pleadingly at him, his eyes begging Sam not to let go.

"I've got you, Sam," Eva yelled, as she strained forward and began to draw them both in, bit by bit, Sam's grasp keeping Alex from sliding out into the void. The wind buffeted them around and Sam started to feel faint from the effort and motion.

Finally Alex reached the webbing and he got a purchase, his legs still dangling out where the wall used to be. Eva clung tightly to them both. Sam could see that up close, her black-lined eyes shone bright-blue, her expression as determined as anyone's he'd seen.

"Yeah!" Alex yelled through gritted teeth. "Nothing to worry about at all!"

His face was all exhaustion and confusion.

"I said," Eva replied, "that we don't die!"

Sam looked out the window on their side—they all did. The helicopter continued to fall, belly first, spinning around and around. The horizon was packed with houses and trees in a vision that was spinning around them in a blur. Sam was sure that in seconds they would become some quiet suburban street's new traffic hazard.

"How?" Alex asked. "What can we do?"

They looked at each other in silence and Sam knew there was nothing they could do. There was no way they could jump for it, if that was supposed to be their way out. Sam looked into Eva's shining, frightened eyes. *I wonder if those eyes will be the last things I'll ever see.*

He took a deep breath and held on tight to them both. The world went silent.

Three . . . two . . . one.

They hit hard.

07

Sam saw bright, blinding light. He squinted against it and then a shadow moved across his vision, eclipsing the harsh assault on his senses, and the world came into focus. Alex, propped up next to Sam, looked down at him, grinning.

Sam could see Alex's mouth move but it took a while for sound to register.

"You OK?"

"I think so . . ." Sam replied. He yawned out his popped ears and his hearing returned nearer to normal levels. Then he noticed he was soaking wet. So was Alex. "How are we not toast right now?"

Alex pointed.

He looked up from where he lay and saw that Eva was standing there, watching him, as stunned as he by the result. She was drenched too, and breathing heavily.

"She pulled me out of the wreck and then we fished you out," Alex said.

"Thanks," Sam said, shell-shocked from the ordeal.

Behind them, the helicopter was steaming and hissing

in a large backyard pool. A mother with a kid on her hip watched on from the safety of her family room, wide-eyed and mouth agape as she stared out the glass doors. Two soldiers, still able-bodied, were pulling their unconscious comrades out of the water and onto the grass.

With the help of his newfound allies, Sam struggled up and got to his feet, where he wobbled unsteadily for a moment.

"That was . . . wow," was all Sam could manage.

"We should so be dead," Alex mused, pouring water out of his shoes. "Human jam for some emergency crew to come scrape off the road."

"That's disgusting," Eva said.

"We've got to get out of here . . ." Sam said, his voice hushed. It wouldn't be long until the soldiers noticed them. They had to escape while they could.

That's when they heard the screeching of tires—it sounded like a convoy of vehicles coming to an abrupt stop in the street in front of the house.

"Someone's here," Sam said, moving towards the sound to take a look, expecting to see emergency crews, the police or some fire engines. He tried to find a good angle from behind the tall fence to see the commotion out on the street, but it was difficult with his hands still bound together. Alex found a piece of jagged steel from the wreck to cut through the plastic binds on Sam's wrists. The three of them climbed up on a rail of the fence and looked over.

Several figures were running fast towards them. They were in plainclothes—certainly not the emergency-crew uniforms Sam hoped to see. Sam fell back from the fence, dragging Eva and Alex with him. The three of them dropped to the ground and rolled towards the cover of the jungle-like garden.

Moments later, a couple of huge guys smashed through the side gate and drew weapons.

Before anyone in the backyard could react, shots rang out.

Sam glanced up and saw that the pilots and soldiers from the helicopter were each being shot, one by one. *Shot with darts*, he realized. They were little feathered things that made a thudding noise as they stuck into bare skin, rendering their targets unconscious.

A tap at Sam's shoulder caused him to jump with fright.

Stunned, he turned and stared at the woman disbelievingly. Alex and Eva hunched in close behind him.

"My name is Lora," she said.

Sam couldn't move. Lora . . . she was *the* Lora, from his dream. She was dressed in tight black clothes, with knee-high boots and black gloves. She held a dart gun in one hand, while the other reached down towards him, as if offering to pull him to his feet.

"We're here to help you," Lora continued.

A group of serious-looking guys, with dart pistols drawn, formed a defensive perimeter. They all wore sunglasses and in-ear radios and resembled undercover secret agents dressed in casual street clothes.

"Who are you guys?" Sam had found his voice again.

"Please, we've no time to waste," Lora pleaded with them. Her flame-red hair blew in the breeze. She took her sunglasses off. She looked *exactly* as she had in Sam's dream. *But, if Lora is real, does that also mean my dream could come true like Eva's?* And after that nightmare ride in the helicopter, he knew he didn't need to pinch himself to be sure he was awake: this was *real*. "Come with us and we'll explain everything on the way."

"On the way to *where*?" Sam persisted.

"Somewhere safe," Lora replied. "Please, follow me."

"Ah, yeah, thanks anyway, but I think we'll be waiting for the cops," Alex said.

Eva looked warily around, not knowing who they should trust.

"Believe me, the police won't be able to protect you— not from them," Lora gestured to the now unconscious soldiers.

Sirens screamed in the distance as Lora gestured for them to move. Cautiously, they followed her to the street, where she held open the rear door of an SUV. The darkened windows and bulk of the car made it look like a tank.

"I guess anyone who is an enemy of those kidnappers is a friend of ours, right?" Eva said as they moved to the car.

"What, you didn't dream this part?" Alex asked her.

Eva shook her head.

"Well, we'll see," Alex said.

"Hurry," Lora replied, and then turned to her armed

companions and said, "let's move to Site B. Stop for no one."

The driver stared at Sam in the rearview mirror. His eyes were like black beetles and his big shaved head sat atop the thick neck and massive shoulders of a wrestler. There was some insignia on his jacket, a symbol containing a horse on a shield.

"He looks just like his picture," the driver said to Lora. Sam frowned. *My picture? How long has all this been planned?*

"Keep your eyes on the road," Lora said to the driver, as she sat in the passenger seat and scanned the residential streets. "And don't lose our detail."

An identical SUV shadowed their moves as they merged onto the highway and headed into the city, going faster than any of the other cars. *Who are these guys?*

Sam's head was spinning and he felt as though he was in some kind of dream—he'd seen Lora in his nightmare last night, and now here she was. *No doubt about it.* He kept it to himself for the moment, although the desire to share it with Eva was overwhelming. *This is too weird.*

"Where are we going?" Sam asked, the first of a million questions swirling around his brain.

"Someplace safe," Lora answered.

"And you are?" Alex asked her.

"I'm the person who's going to make sure you stay safe," she said, and turned around in her seat to face the three of them. "There are plenty more like those Agents back there who will stop at nothing to get to the three of you."

The teenagers shared a look, and Alex leaned forward and said, "I'm Alex, and—"

"Yes, I know," Lora said. "We can save small talk for later."

"I wasn't introducing myself to be polite," he said. "I want to know exactly who *you* are and *where* we're going."

Lora was silent. She kept looking out the windows as though that was far more important than Alex's questions.

"How?" Sam asked her. "*How* do you know who we are? And what did your driver here mean when he said I look just like my picture? Why would you have my picture?"

Lora smiled. "Sam, that's a long story—"

"Well, try me!" Sam interjected. "Please, give us something."

"OK, we know what you look like because we've been keeping an eye on you. On all of you. Through a friendly source. And that's all I can say for now," Lora said with finality. "We have to get off the streets first; we have to go someplace secure. Then, we can talk all you want."

"We don't have to *get* anywhere," Alex said. "I want to know what's going on—now!"

"OK . . ." Lora said, letting out a loud exhale, though her eyes were still scanning out the car's windows for threats.

Sam waited expectantly.

"Put simply?" Lora said, her voice quiet and matter-of-fact. "The three of you are being hunted."

"Hunted? What, like animals?" Eva asked.

Lora nodded.

"By who," Alex asked, "those guys back there?"

"Them, and pretty soon everyone else."

"Why us?" Sam asked.

"Because right now, the three of you are some of the most valuable people in the world."

Valuable? Sam thought. *What are we? Things to be bought and sold?*

"Some will stop at nothing to get their hands on you," Lora continued.

"Were those soldiers back there from the government?"

Alex asked.

The driver laughed.

"I mean, with helicopters like that, they've gotta be, right?" Alex said.

"And at my school they said something about national security," Sam added.

"Mine too!" Eva said.

"All these *hows* and *whys* will be answered in detail, I promise," Lora said. "And as for those guys back there, they're not from any government."

"How about you?" Sam asked.

Lora shook her head. "We're not from the government either—but know this: we *are* the good guys."

Alex laughed disbelievingly.

"They picked us up out of school," Eva said. "Why would they—I mean, *who* could do that?"

Lora looked forward again as the car took a sharp turn to pass a truck, then turned back to reply. "They're from an outfit known as the Enterprise."

"The what?" Sam asked.

"Slow down," Lora said to the driver, as a police car cruised by.

Alex made as though he was going to signal them.

"Look, my dad's a cop, so you better—" he faltered as the driver laughed again. Lora shot the guy a look and Alex said, "Something funny, big guy?"

The driver looked like he wanted to fire something back

but he was busy navigating the downtown exit from the freeway.

"Why are we in such a hurry?" Eva asked.

"Because they'll be coming after us," Lora replied, looking out the windows as she spoke. "They're never far behind."

"The Enterprise, you mean?" Sam asked.

Lora nodded. Alex sniggered incredulously, and Sam and Eva looked at him, unnerved. Sam again considered sharing his dream, about how he'd seen this Lora woman before, especially given that Eva's dream about the helicopter had become real just moments ago. But it all seemed too much, too unbelievable. *What if this woman isn't the ally she appeared to be in my dream?* He swallowed hard against the rising bile in his throat.

"What about that missile that shot us down?" Sam asked. "Did you do that?"

"No," Lora replied, with a flash of anxiety on her face. "That's the most worrying thing about all this, Sam—I have no idea who would have done that to the Enterprise, or to you . . ."

Sam watched as their convoy pulled into the basement parking garage of a massive high-rise. The place looked ordinary enough and he was relieved to see plenty of people coming and going. Drivers occasionally tooted as their urgent, speeding SUVs kept heading downward, the tires squealing on the smooth concrete floor as they twisted along the ramps, until they came to the almost-empty lowest basement level. Their driver touched his earpiece and turned to Lora.

"Details of the helicopter incident have gone public," he said as the cars braked to a hard stop near an exit door and elevator. "The police won't be far behind the Enterprise Agents."

"Then we're going to have to move faster than we thought," Lora said. They got out, the other vehicles spewing six guys, each as big and serious as the next. "Torch the cars; we're never coming back here."

Sam looked around the basement for a way out—there was an elevator and a couple of stairwells, all of them too far to make a run for it. He noticed the men were now armed with little snub-nosed machine guns. Two guys were busy attaching explosives to the underside of the cars. *This is insane!*

Lora led the way to the elevator, where she pressed the call button. She turned and faced Sam, Eva and Alex, who remained steadfast by the cars. She walked back over and stopped up close.

"Look," Lora said. "I am the best option the three of you have right now."

Sam saw the others both looked as nervous and scared as he was.

"Sam, Eva, Alex," Lora said, her tone friendly, "I *know* this is hard, to trust me so soon, but think about it: if we meant you harm, we'd have left you back there at the crash site."

"She's got a point," Eva said.

"Are you kidding?" Alex exclaimed. "What, are you with them or something?"

Eva flinched. "None of this makes any more sense to me than you."

Alex turned to Lora. "I want you to take us to a police station," he said.

"You wouldn't be safe there."

"Not safe in a police station?" Alex said, incredulous.

"I think she means, not safe from *them*," Sam said.

"Who *are* they, these Enterprise people? I mean, you're telling us they're above the law?" Eva said, glaring at Alex and Lora in turn. "I don't understand what's going on—and I really want to."

They all jumped as squealing tires from a few levels above echoed through the garage.

"That'll be Enterprise Agents," Lora said, "but the unknown people who shot down your helicopter are the ones I'm really worried about right now because we don't know who they are or what they want, beyond your demise. If they find us down here, we're sitting ducks. Listen, my guys and I will fight to the *death* to protect the three of you—and maybe then you'll believe what I've said about us being here to help you."

Their driver walked over and whispered into her ear. Lora nodded as he and the other guys ran towards the up ramp.

The elevator pinged, the doors opened.

Lora got in and turned towards the three uncertain teens. "This is your last chance. If you stay here, they will have you. You come with me, you live another day."

"We'll—we'll take our chances—"

"No chances," Lora said to Alex, holding the doors open. "No doubt: whoever shot your helicopter down with a missile wanted you dead and for all we know, it could be them above us in this parking garage right now."

The sound of tires screeching was growing closer—then there came the rip-patter of machine-gun fire, a crash of steel-on-steel and a concussive explosion echoed around them.

Eva rushed into the elevator. Lora nodded at her, and then looked at Sam.

Sam turned to Alex, and said, "I guess we've got no choice," and together they entered the elevator. The doors closed behind them. Lora inserted a key into a panel and opened it to reveal a numerical keypad, where she entered a code and the elevator went down, *far*.

10

The elevator doors opened to reveal a long, dimly lit corridor. Lora hastily led them down it, their hurried noises reverberating off the solid concrete walls and ceiling. They came to a room with a massive steel door and another code was entered. The door clunked open and a cold wind sucked in and around them, making them shiver. Rows of neon lights blinked into life—but that was the only modern touch. Sam couldn't believe his eyes.

They stood on what looked like an old underground subway station, carved out of the rock. Dust and cobwebs coated everything.

"Whoa," Alex said, "so this isn't getting weirder at all."

Lora spoke quietly into her phone. Sam strained to hear but she turned away. He checked his own phone—no signal.

"This whole day's been getting more unbelievable by the second," Sam said quietly to Alex and Eva. "Supposed 'national security' armed men picking us up."

"Loading us onto a helicopter," Eva added.

"Getting shot from the sky," Alex said. "And you seeing it in a dream." He looked at Eva with narrowed eyes.

"*Surviving* the crash landing . . ." Eva said meaningfully.

"All of it," Alex conceded, "it's doing my head in."

Sam thought back to his own dream. He looked at Lora. *I wonder if she remembers being in my dream?* He shook himself free of the foolish thought.

"Maybe, right now, we're all still dreaming," Eva said.

"I can assure you," Lora said, standing before them, her phone back on her belt, next to a holstered dart gun, "you're not dreaming."

A train appeared in the dark tunnel. Silent but for a quiet hum on the tracks, its headlights were the only telltale sign of the approach. It was small, about a third of the size of a regular subway car. Super sleek, its nose was sharp, like a bullet train. It didn't have a driver, or any passengers.

"Our ride," Lora said, walking towards it and entering through the sliding doors that opened on her approach.

Sam looked at the others.

"Why stop now?" he said, and led the way aboard.

"I'm tagging along only because I want more answers," Alex frowned, following Sam. Eva paused only a moment longer before she chose not to be left behind.

The trip was fully automated. The doors shut and then they took off down the tracks, the headlights lighting up what looked like any other subway tunnel. Inside, there was enough seating for a dozen people. Up front was a small control panel. No sooner had they left the platform than it seemed like they were traveling at a hundred miles per hour, the tunnel flashing by and the tracks rattling beneath them.

"This another part that you didn't dream about?" Alex said to Eva, noting the worry on her face.

"I don't like dark tunnels," she replied. "And no, I didn't see any of this—my dream ended at the crash landing."

"You dreamed that?" Lora asked Eva, leaning across to her, her eyes intense.

"Yes . . ." Eva hesitantly replied.

"When?"

"Last night. I mean, I dream most nights, but this one was . . . it came true . . ."

Eva's voice trailed off and Sam could see that she was caught up in the memory of it, as he'd been about his own nightmare this morning.

"You're saying," Lora said, choosing her words deliberately, "that you dreamed about the *exact* events leading up to the helicopter ride?"

Eva nodded. "Up to and including, yeah."

"Have your dreams done that before?" Lora asked.

"Done what?"

"Have they come true?" Sam said for Lora. "That's what you want to know, isn't it? If she's some kind of, what, a prophet or something?"

"In a sense, yes," Lora agreed, eyeing Sam carefully.

Eva shook her head. "Only my last dream came true and it was all so real, all of the details, right down to meeting Sam and Alex."

Alex shook his head as if all of this was crazy. Sam swallowed hard, wondering how this figured into his own recent vivid dream. *If that comes true . . .*

"And you dreamed what, exactly?" Lora asked.

"Everything that happened," Eva replied. "I dreamed it all, from being picked up out of my dorm room, to meeting these two and then being shot from the sky. Everything up until we stood there, by the pool, dripping wet."

Sam watched Lora's reactions. *She seems worried by this,* he thought.

"Every bit of it played out exactly as I dreamed it," Eva continued. "*Exactly.*"

Lora still looked like she was lost in thought.

"Do you know how that could have happened?" Sam asked Lora.

Lora's focus shifted from the middle distance to Eva then settled on Sam.

"Did you dream last night too?"

Sam hesitated, and then nodded. Lora looked scared to ask more, but she did.

Slowly, she said, "Sam, what did you dream?"

The three of them looked at Sam. So he took a deep breath and told them, just as he'd told his parents. He told them of the masked man, the crystal sphere, the flash of light and fire, and the horror of all those lives lost. He shared every detail but for one thing: he left out that Lora was there. He wanted to know more about her first, needed to know if he could trust her. Plus it was unnerving, having his dream, his *nightmare*, become that much more . . . *possible*, now that he'd met her, now that he'd lived Eva's dream. When he finished recounting his story, Lora's face was pale.

"Sorry if it was a bit graphic," Sam said, feeling guilty for sharing the dread and fear he felt. "It was just a dream, right?"

Alex and Eva looked tense. There was silence but for the electric motor whining underneath the train car and the tracks rattling out the tune of their immense speed.

"One question, Sam," Lora said. "Are you particularly bothered by any part of that dream?"

"Ah, aside from the creepy figure dressed all in black that killed everyone?"

"I mean, do you have a phobia of mysterious figures like that, or cafes or crowds or something?" Lora continued. "I know that sounds strange but what I'm asking is: does anything in your dream have a personal meaning to you?"

"Phobia of cafes? That's the weirdest thing you've said yet," Sam joked. But he looked at her serious expression, and nodded his head to concede the point. "OK, yeah, the fire. I'm scared of fire."

"Is it something that happened?" Lora asked, her voice soft and caring.

Sam shifted uncomfortably.

"It's important, Sam. You can talk about it some other time if you like, but it would really help to know what you're thinking." Lora's eyes were kind, reminding him of his mother's.

But Sam couldn't do it; he couldn't talk about what had happened to Bill. He shook his head.

"Well, don't be scared," Lora said, although the expression on her face seemed to say otherwise. "This nightmare you had, we won't let that happen."

Who's we? Sam thought. But he let it go for the moment, as he could tell her reassurance wasn't just for him, or Eva or Alex; it was also for Lora herself.

11

"This is our stop," Lora said, getting herself ready as the train slowed of its own accord.

"Where are we?" Eva asked.

"This track runs through disused sections of subway lines, abandoned mine shafts and sewer systems," Lora said.

"Sewer?" Eva said. "Ergh. That's disgusting."

"We set it up years ago when we had a base nearby," Lora said. "No one knows about it, which means we're able to get across town undetected."

They stopped at another small underground platform and the doors opened.

"No one knows about this," Alex said, "except for . . ."

Lora turned to him, the question obvious, but Alex finished it anyway.

". . . you guys . . . whoever you are . . ."

"It took you this long to ask?" a man said, walking into view from the darkened recess of the platform. He was tall, with blond hair and steel-gray eyes, probably in his late twenties. *Man, this guy looks like an action-movie hero.* Lora embraced him warmly but his eyes stayed on Sam.

"My name's Sebastian," the guy said. "Lora and I work at the Academy, which is explanation enough for now. What's important is for you to understand that we need to get you to safety as quickly as possible. There are dangerous forces that will stop at nothing to get their hands on the three of you."

Sam and his two companions stood on the platform, suddenly united in their confusion and caution. He could tell that they'd all come to the same conclusion—that there was little they could do right now but go along with Lora and Sebastian. In the dim light ahead, a door opened, revealing another elevator. The five of them entered—Lora, Eva and Alex first, Sam and Sebastian at the rear. This time there was just one button for Lora to press: UP.

"You're saying that this Enterprise group wants to kill us?" Alex asked.

"They don't want to kill you," Lora said.

"But he said that they—"

"They want to take you in. Capture you."

"They tried to blow us up!" Alex said.

Lora turned to Sebastian, who continued to watch Sam as though he were gazing at some kind of exotic fish in an aquarium. She explained, "Someone fired a missile at their heli—"

"I know," Sebastian said, as the elevator rose. "It's all over the news, some civilians caught the impact on camera. This is moving faster than we'd predicted. Here, take a look at this."

Sebastian handed Lora his phone, showing a news report of the crash.

The elevator journey was quick. The doors opened and they walked towards a sleek jet parked inside a hangar, its engines already whirring for takeoff.

"No way," Eva said, pausing at the base of the stairs leading up to the jet. "I can't. I'm not going any further until we know exactly who you are and what's going on. Our parents must be freaking out by now; we need to speak to them. This is crazy!"

Sebastian looked from Lora to the three of them.

"I'm with Eva," said Alex, crossing his arms. "We still don't know squat. How do we know what you've said isn't all a pack of lies? Maybe the Enterprise are the good guys and you're not. Sam, you with us?"

Sam didn't need to answer. He stood next to the two of them with quiet resolve.

Sebastian's look softened. He walked over to them and Sam felt relieved that the guy was finally going to lay it all out: *who* they were, *why* they were here, *what* this whole big mess was about. *Finally, some answers!*

Instead, Sebastian pulled a gun out from under his jacket, smiled coldly, and fired at Eva and Alex. Sam gasped and lunged forward for the weapon as darts stabbed into their chests. But he was too late—Sebastian had turned the gun on him and fired. The dart made his eyes water and he watched helplessly as the grimy concrete floor came up to meet his face.

12

"**S**am?"

Sam drifted in and out of consciousness. He saw the cream-colored world of the interior of the jet and slipped back into the black fog of unconsciousness and then further into a world of dreams. He saw a night's sky, and for a moment he felt as though he was flying above a city street.

"Sam?"

He knew it was the dream world that he'd been tumbling in and out of. It was some kind of in-between state of being awake and asleep; it felt dangerous. The kind of dream where he knew he should be alert; it was *important*, but there was nothing he could do about it. There were noises around him, foreign, mechanical, close and then fading to the distance. He saw a face above him and then fell back into another dream where he was aboard an aircraft.

"Sam, wake up!" a woman's voice said, her voice familiar. "Seb, how much did you give him?"

"Mom?" Sam said in delirium. Then his eyes flickered open, the world around him painted in between blinks. "Where am I?"

There were two people sitting close to him. It took a moment for him to recall their names.

"Alex? Eva?"

"Hey, sleepyhead," Eva said. "Are you OK?"

Sam mumbled, "Yeah," lifted his head, felt dizzy, and took a moment to steady himself. He looked around. They were inside the cabin of a small jet.

"Sam, we're about to land," Alex said.

Land? Sam rubbed his neck. The pain of falling onto the concrete shuddered through him. Alex had a grazed bump on his forehead and fire in his eyes. He was staring hard at Sebastian, watching as the man closed a laptop, looked out the window and then turned around to face them— nonchalant, like it was any other day.

"Buckle up," Sebastian said.

Alex looked at Sam. "And before you ask, I've already tried to find out from the tough guy here why he had to dart us like that."

"Tried?"

"He's the silent type, apparently."

Sebastian ignored them and carried on packing away his work.

"Where are we landing?" Sam asked, figuring that Alex's approach wasn't going to get them very far. He wondered if there'd be any potential for escape when the trip was over. But still no answers came from Sebastian.

Lora joined them. She passed around bottled water then sat down, buckling into the spare seat opposite Sam.

"I'm really very sorry about all that," Lora said, helping Sam straighten his plush recliner chair. "You feeling OK?"

Sam nodded.

"We're about to land in Switzerland."

"What?" Sam said, looking out the window at the cloudy sky and back to Lora. *Snow, ice and mountains . . . great. It's going to have to be one amazing escape plan to get out of this.* "How long was I out?"

"A few hours."

"A few hours?" Sam tried to calculate. "And we're already over Switzerland?"

"It's a fast plane," Lora said. "In five minutes you'll be meeting the others, getting all the answers you're after and then some."

"Others?" Sam looked at Eva and Alex, but he could tell that they were none the wiser—so he obviously hadn't missed anything important while he'd been out cold.

"And, ah, where are we landing, exactly?" Sam sipped his water, feeling more awake by the second.

"There, look," Lora said and pointed out the small window between them. As the aircraft broke through the cloud cover, the snowy tops of mountains sparkled close below. The blanket of white was interspersed with patches of gray rocks and rubble.

"There's nowhere to land," Eva said, looking out her own window. "There's no way we can touch down . . ."

The jet dived down fast. Sam got a glimpse of their destination as they banked into their landing approach: a small collection of ancient-looking stone-walled buildings on top of a craggy mountain. But there was no runway, just the rocky snowcapped ridge. He tightened his seatbelt.

13

The jet engines roared in Sam's ears and the cabin shook as the pilot eased the aircraft downward. They were now flying vertically, switching from horizontal flight to hover like a helicopter above the landing site. Sam craned his neck to see sheer cliffs only a few feet away from the sides and rear of the jet. *This is crazy, we're not going to make it!* Sam looked at Lora and Sebastian, sitting calmly in their seats, feeling anything but calm himself as the aircraft touched down with little more than a bump. Lora ushered them out and Sam glanced back at the jet as he stumbled away, surprised his eyes weren't left somewhere in the rear of the plane.

"Follow me!" Lora yelled over the wind. "The weather's turning!"

Their group headed for the main building that was far larger than it had appeared from the air. Dense clouds rolled in through the mountains, dark fingers wrapping around the white peaks, the sun low on the horizon and glinting brightly. A tiny, snow-covered road led off to the west. Sam could just make out a helicopter visible in a cave-like hangar on an outcrop to the north. As Sam trudged from the plane's landing pad through the ankle-deep snow, he couldn't help but be in awe. The place seemed to be the ultimate mountaintop secret lair and he had a feeling that things were only going to get more unreal.

"Looks like an old monastery," Eva said to Sam and Alex as the nearing building shielded them from the worst of the gale. It was a long stone structure with a terracotta tiled roof. The windows were high and small, as if to keep the worst of the weather out. The building was hundreds of years old, by the look of it. Warily, they followed Lora and Sebastian to the imposing entrance.

"Hurry!" Lora called back at them. The horizontal sheets of snow started whipping over the roof. They had blown up the side of the mountain and were crashing over the ridge above the building, like a wave.

"What is this place?" Sam asked, squinting against the blinding powder snow.

Lora turned, pausing at the ancient double doors, massive slabs of wood that creaked open as they approached. "This is the heart of the Academy, our school for the gifted."

Sam looked up at a carved sign above the stone lintel.

"It basically means *mind over matter*," Eva translated. Alex looked at her, puzzled. "What, they didn't teach you Latin at your school?"

"I'm lucky I learned English at my school," Alex replied.

As they entered the building, an older man rushed over to greet them. He was wearing a fuzzy knitted sweater the same color as his wispy gray hair. It reminded Sam of his dad's embarrassing Christmas outfits. The old guy smiled and caught his breath.

"Welcome—welcome to the Academy," he said in a deep voice. "I must admit, this day has come earlier than I'd expected, and yet later than we can all afford." He held out his hand to Sam, who shook it, and then did the same with Eva and Alex. "My name is Tom, but the students and staff call me Professor. I'm the headmaster. I am so pleased to see you here at last. If you will follow me, time is of the essence."

The corridors were long, with worn cobbled floors that spoke of the comings and goings of many. The place was teaming with teenage students. All were dressed in ordinary-looking uniforms that had golden emblems on the left side. Sam looked closer and recognized the emblem— it was a dream catcher. The teaching staff wore various shades of red. Many heads turned at the sight of Sam's group as they passed. Most students looked at them curiously, but a few looked afraid.

"This wing is where all our classes take place," the Professor said. "Except for the applied science labs, which are in the reinforced levels below the hangar."

Alex gave Sam and Eva a smirk behind the Professor's back, as if the old man was spinning it.

"I assure you, Alex, it's a necessary precaution," he said and turned around to usher the trio through a doorway. "This is the dining hall."

Sam took a deep breath. The room was vast, and the light through the stained-glass windows gave it an ethereal quality. Stretched above them was a vaulted wood ceiling with massive exposed beams supporting the soccer-field-sized terracotta roof. Thirteen large oval tables, each with seating for about thirty, were lined up along the floor.

"Dinner will be served here in about an hour's time," the Professor said, turning to them and smiling warmly as he checked his watch. "If you'll continue to follow me . . ."

"Wait, Professor," Alex interrupted. "Why are you showing us around? What are we doing here? We need some answers, fast."

"Alex is right," Sam said. "One minute we're shot at—"

"Then drugged by your buddies!" Alex added.

"And now you're showing us around," Sam said, "acting as if this is all . . ."

"All normal!" Alex said. "Which it ain't, let me tell you. I'm usually dozing through my English class about now."

"Of course, I'm sorry, you've had the most tumultuous day, I know. I will do my best to explain all this in a moment—just not here, in the hallway," the Professor replied and looked meaningfully at the throng of students gazing curiously at them. He walked on, but as he turned and waited for the three of them, he realized that they weren't going anywhere without further explanation. "Meanwhile, I thought that you'd at least want to check out the layout of the place so you can hatch a good escape plan as soon as we leave you to your own devices."

The Professor looked kindly at Alex, who had flushed a vibrant shade of red.

Alex swallowed. The three of them followed close behind the Professor, across the hall.

"Where are Sebastian and Lora?" Alex asked Sam from the corner of his mouth, craning around to look for them.

"Disappeared as soon as we entered the building," Sam replied.

"I've gotta say, I'm not going to miss that guy. Now that he's gone, I figure we'll hear what this old guy, the Professor or whatever, has to say and if it still stinks we'll demand to be taken to the closest embassy and then they'll sort out how to get us home."

"Or we sneak out—"

"Shh!" Eva said, and the boys fell silent.

They'd walked to the back of the hall, and through a wooden door into an amphitheater. The room was fitted out with plush theater-style seating in curved rows scaled down the steep incline of the room. There must have been about two hundred seats or more, behind the top tier of which was an expanse of carpeted floor that led to large, glazed double doors. Poking his head through the doors, Sam could see an outside deck that appeared to float at the edge of a cliff face. The feeling of standing on something that, by a trick of architecture, felt unsupported and looking out over the tallest mountains he'd ever seen, was enough to break Sam out in a cold sweat.

"You don't like heights?" Eva asked.

"Hadn't really worried about it before," he replied, "but after that helicopter ride . . ."

"This is the social room," the Professor said, pausing in his quick-paced march. "This is where we screen movies, have concerts, guest lectures and so on."

Lora appeared in front of them, at the far end of the room. She'd changed into the red colors of the teaching staff.

"Ah, there you are," the Professor said, and turned to his three prospective students. "Lora has been with us since she was fourteen. One of our best-ever graduates. She is now our operations director."

"The what now?" Alex said.

"I handle the Academy's recruitment," Lora explained, seeming happy to join the procession, back in the direction from where she had come. "Along with other tasks that need to be performed outside the Academy grounds."

"You say recruitment, I say kidnapping . . ."

"Seriously though, you are potential students, Alex, which is why we brought you here. The three of you have talents we would like to help you to realize and develop."

"We'll see . . ." Alex's voice trailed off, then he stopped to let out a whistle. "Whoa, this is amazing!"

Ahead of them, the floor and walls formed a long bridge of clear glass over a jaw-dropping mountain pass, connecting two sections of the Academy. Sam hesitated, trying not to look down at the incomprehensible drop, before gingerly venturing out.

"This leads to our hall of honor," the Professor said. As they walked out onto the glass, the hallway began to fill with lights that changed colors with each step.

"Is this glass—did it just . . ." Eva trailed off. "Is it changing colors to—to suit us?"

"It's spectral glass," Lora explained. "It reads your aura as you pass by, reflecting your . . . gifts."

Around where Lora stood, the glass floor under her feet and the wall behind her was lit up with swirling yellows and oranges and reds. The Professor's colors were darker and it seemed as though solar flares were erupting around his flowing outline. Sam looked over at Eva, who was staring at her hands and arms against the glass, seeing similar colors to Lora's, only not so big or bright. Alex had outlines of blue and green around his body.

"This is cool!" Alex said, shuffling his feet up and down, looking at how the glass reacted with his own special signature of colors.

"Sam?" Eva asked. "What's with your . . ?"

He looked at his feet—they appeared to be on fire. All around him were red and orange leaping flames, with hints of blue and white where the fire burned brightest.

"Get it off me!" he yelled, panicked. "Get it off!"

"It's OK, just keep walking," Lora said, although the hesitation in her voice did little to put Sam at ease. "The hall is different for everyone who walks it. Keep walking and look straight ahead. You'll be all right. It's just lights, they can't hurt you."

Sam ran across the remainder of the bridge, looking straight ahead, not down.

The others crossed the bridge in silence, and as they reached the solid stone floor on the other side, Lora held back from the others, and stopped in front of Sam.

"Can you tell me now, about the fire?" she asked.

"I . . . no," Sam said. "Why is this called the hall of honor?"

He walked around Lora, anxious to break away from the awkward moment.

"Because of these," the Professor said, as the hall opened up to a bigger space of stark white walls. A gallery of portraits hung along either side.

"Who are these photos of?" Eva asked.

"They're paintings, actually," the Professor said.

"Really?" Eva said. She looked closely, as did Sam and Alex. They could see that each portrait really was painted by hand. Each of them was the size of a door, and there were at least fifty lining the walls.

"This is incredible," Sam said, transfixed by a painting of a girl not much older than himself, although she was dressed in old-fashioned clothes. Close up, the painting looked almost pixelated, and it took a moment for Sam to realize that it was made up of thousands of smaller pictures. "How do they . . ?"

Each little square was a smaller painting of a face, interspersed with tiny images of mechanical gears. Some of the faces were familiar—famous scientists, artists and inventors. Others were unknown, but there seemed to be some connection in the expressions—*were some of these people family members?*

"Pretty neat, huh?" Lora said.

"They're amazing," Eva said.

"Who are these portraits of?" Alex asked.

The Professor stopped before the last of the portraits and turned to it. The name *Isaac Newton* was on a plaque underneath.

"Each portrait depicts a talented person who, over the last few thousand years, has made a significant contribution to our world," he explained. "Back in Ancient Greece, there were people like Plato and Hypatia—both respected philosophers and mathematicians. And of course, in the time of the Renaissance, there was Leonardo da Vinci, one of this world's finest minds—an artist, scientist, inventor . . . and Isaac Newton you may have studied in school," the Professor glanced at Sam as he pointed to the portrait. "Albert Einstein, Wolfgang Mozart, Marie Curie, Stephen Hawking . . . a few names you may or may not have heard of, but there are many others."

They started walking again, and passed some blank canvases.

"Why are some blank?" Eva asked.

"They're for future additions," Lora said. "*Dreamers*, as we like to call them."

"Sam?" Eva said. Sam was staring intently at a blank canvas. He shifted from left to right, thinking it was a trick, but it wasn't—he was looking at a painting of himself. "How . . ?"

Then, in the blink of an eye, it changed to the masked face from Sam's nightmare. There and gone again so quick Sam could not be sure if he had even seen it.

As Lora came over to see, the painting remained blank.

"How did it do that?" he wondered out loud. "Did anyone see that?"

"What did you see, Sam?" Eva asked.

"The masked man!" Sam said. "I saw him, the one from my dream. How could that be?"

Lora touched his arm. "I didn't see anything, Sam. But one of the first things that you'll learn here at the Academy is that nightmares, whether they come true or not, are powerful. Your mind is probably trying to work through the trauma of the last day, and you've projected the image onto the canvas."

Sam was comforted for a moment, but as they turned to continue on, he struggled to get his breathing under control and couldn't shake the feeling that there wasn't anything normal about any of this. Worse still, the most unusual thing here seemed to be him—him, and his nightmares, and the phrase that Lora had just spoken: *whether they come true or not.*

14

Lora continued to give them the tour along their way to the Professor's office, as the Professor went ahead to attend to some business.

"You know," Lora said as she led them up a spiral staircase, "I remember when I was new here. I know it's quite mind-bending at first."

"That's the understatement of the century," Eva said.

"Well, I promise you this: the payoff is well worth it." Lora stopped at the landing at the top of the stairs, in a waiting room full of comfy couches and armchairs. "Make no mistake—your lives have changed forever."

Alex rolled his eyes again and stayed cross-eyed, Sam nearly choking with laughter.

Through the open doors was a small room with a lady seated behind a desk, busily typing away. She reminded Sam of his grandmother.

"You may go in," the woman said, her eyes following them discreetly as they passed.

The Professor's office was an oval room that wrapped around the cliff face, the rough-hewn rock forming one of the walls. There was a wide picture window looking out to the mountains that stretched into the distance. Ancient artifacts lined the walls in display cases and on shelves—Egyptian, Mayan, Greek, Chinese . . . it looked like a mini-museum.

Two giant, Himalayan mountain dogs, black, brown and white balls of fur with big happy faces, sprang to life and ran up to Lora for a scratch behind the ears, then padded over to sniff the three new arrivals.

"Gee, great guard dogs," Alex whispered under his breath.

"Welcome, welcome, please, come in," the Professor said as soon as he ended his phone call. "Would you like a drink?"

Sam suddenly realized how thirsty he was, running his tongue over his dry lips. Alex and Eva evidently had the same thought.

The Professor smiled and pointed across the room to a drink cart. "Help yourselves."

Sam poured sodas for them all, which they gulped down noisily and Alex gave a satisfied burp.

"A side effect of the dart's drug," Lora said to them. "The thirst I mean, not the belching."

Alex peeled off another deep, satisfied burp.

"I don't know," he said. "I think it made me pretty gassy."

"Please, sit," the Professor said, motioning to some chairs across from his ancient wooden desk—an artifact in itself it seemed. Lora sat at the Professor's side and stirred a cup of tea.

"So, fire away," the Professor said. "You must have a hundred questions, and hopefully I can answer them all."

Try a million, Sam thought, though he didn't know where to start. They rushed through his mind in a flash: *What is all this about? Why were we brought here? Who are these Dreamers? Why were people after them?*

The Professor smiled at him.

"OK, I'll start," Sam said, seeing that his companions were at least as overwhelmed as he. "What is this place?"

"This is the Academy's main campus," the Professor replied.

"And the Academy is *what*, exactly?" Sam asked.

"It is a school for some of the world's most gifted minds," Lora said.

"So it's just a special school?" Eva said. "That's *it*?"

"Our students are encouraged to be the best that they can be," the Professor said, "so that they may achieve their dreams, and beyond. We'd like you all to have that same opportunity, to join us." He leaned forward, his arms crossed on the desk. "However, first I have something difficult to tell you. The people you have all known as your parents? Well . . . there's no easy way to put this, so I'll just say it—they are not who you think they are."

15

Sam sat stunned as he tried to comprehend what he'd just been told.

"You're saying . . ."

"I'm saying," the Professor said slowly, "your parents are not your *biological* parents."

"I *knew* it," said Alex with deadpan sarcasm. "That so makes sense! I mean, they're aliens, right? They've gotta be. Probably my dog too, right? I bet he's able to turn into some kind of beast to protect me from space lizards."

Alex laughed as if he'd told the world's most hilarious joke while Sam rubbed his temples, processing what he'd heard about his parents. Eva was silent, dumbstruck.

"But that means," Sam said, "not only are my parents *not* my parents, but that Ben isn't my brother?"

Lora nodded.

"This is unbelievable," Sam said.

The Professor and Lora shared an uncomfortable look.

"If they're not our parents," Eva asked, her voice shaky, "then who are they?"

"Eva," Lora said. "I know this is hard to hear, but they're actually Enterprise Agents."

"Their job was to raise you as their own," the Professor said. "To look after you, guide you, to observe."

"Observe what?" Eva said.

"Your dreams," Lora said. "To see if you could be guided to have *true* dreams. But they didn't know the half of it . . ."

"Hold on a minute, let me get this straight. My parents—*all* of our parents," Sam said, pointing to the other two, "are *Agents*, working for the *Enterprise*?"

"Yes," the Professor replied.

Sam stood up and started to pace the room. "Right. And what does that mean, Lora, *true* dreams?"

"Dreams like Eva had last night," Lora said, "where the dream predicts upcoming events. That potential is why this morning played out like it did."

Sam felt nauseous.

"I know this is a lot to take in," Lora said, sitting forward and passing Eva a tissue to wipe the tears from her eyes. "I'm so sorry, Eva. The Agents' job is to raise a potential Dreamer as their own child, caring for them, watching them, reporting on them constantly."

"And then what?" Eva asked.

"If and when they start dreaming, not as everyone else does, but as *Dreamers*—as you did last night, Eva—then they are turned over to work with the Enterprise." Lora let the silence hang in the room.

"You need to keep in mind that while we disagree with the Enterprise's tactics and vision, their Agents are not bad people," the Professor said. "They don't mean you harm. They did what they thought was right."

"You're saying that they were just doing a job . . ." Sam said, then glanced across to Lora. "But all the photos of me as a kid—my mom even has photos of me at the hospital with her, when I was born. And ultrasounds. What about all that?"

"I don't know, but for many of them, caring for the potential Dreamer is not a pretense for long," Lora said. "In most cases the Agent parents are as emotionally involved as any parent is with their child."

"Which is why they are often reluctant to let the Enterprise know when the true dreaming starts, as they know they will lose their child," the Professor added. "So they are watched very carefully by their superiors."

"Your parents wouldn't have had a choice in handing you over," Lora added. "They were doing their job, as we here at the Academy do ours. '

"Which is?" Sam asked.

"To protect you, to teach you," the Professor said. "And help guide you through the race ahead."

"The race?" Something triggered in Sam's mind. "You mean a race to find the last 13."

"Yes," the Professor's eyes twinkled keenly. "When did you dream that?"

"Last night," Sam said. He sat down in the chair next to Alex and Eva, and could see them looking to him for answers. "But I don't know what the 13 are. Objects? People?"

"People. But we'll get to that shortly." The Professor seemed reluctant though to continue.

"I just can't believe this," Eva said, her mind still stuck in the bombshell of a minute ago. "My *parents* . . . my *family* . . . they're not—they're not really *mine* . . ."

"Me too." Alex threw his hands in the air. "I mean, what's next? You're going to tell us that the Easter Bunny is real, that he lives with the Big Bad Wolf and they're hatching some evil plot to take over the world?"

The Professor gave a nod to Lora, who in turn pressed a button on her phone and placed it on the desk.

"Sam," Lora said, "I'm sorry to do this, but you all need to listen to a recording of a phone call. It was made this morning."

Sam's waited, anxious.

There was a clicking sound over the tiny speaker—*a telephone being picked up.*

A male voice said, "Enterprise."

"Agent Emergency, coding in."

Sam recognized his mother's voice, his *fake mother's* voice, right away.

"Go ahead," the man's voice said.

Sam listened as Jane replied with a series of numbers

and answered three security questions in quick succession.

The operator said, "Confirmed. What is your situation?"

Jane's voice shook, ever so slightly, as she said, "Sam has activated. And I think he might be one of the last 13."

"The last 13?" said the guy on the other end. He sounded incredulous. "Confirm, one-three, thirteen?"

"Yes, 13. He needs to be taken in."

Sam could hear other phones ringing in the background, like a whole switchboard was lighting up at the Enterprise.

"This is what we've been waiting for," Jane continued. "He dreamed about the prophecy. And I think he saw *him*. You know what that means—the 13 Dreamers are readying—the race has started . . . maybe I should speak to a senior Agent."

"I'm the most senior Agent here."

"OK, then you know the protocol. The Dreamer must be collected for processing."

Agent? Dreamer? Sam thought with a sinking feeling. *It's all true!*

The phones in the background of wherever the operator was were a symphony now.

He said, "You know that can't be undone."

There was a pause and then Sam's mother said with sadness, "I know."

"After that," Lora said, pausing the recording, "they organized for the rather dramatic helicopter pickup at your school. We have similar intercepts from Eva's and Alex's homes too."

The room was silent. Eva looked at Sam through tearful eyes.

"If that's right," Eva said, "then who are our real parents?"

"And where are they?" Sam added.

"I'm afraid that's something we don't yet know," Lora said, glancing at the Professor. "But we will help you find out."

Eva hesitated. "Can . . . can I hear the recording of my parents?"

Lora played the recorded conversation from Eva's house, all of it similar to Sam's although there was no mention of a masked man.

"OK," Eva said, swallowing hard. The expression on her face showed that the world as she knew it had just been pulled out from under her feet. "OK. I believe you. I believe it all."

Then it was Alex's turn. As the recording began to play, his Enterprise Agent mother coding in, Alex jumped out of his seat.

"That's enough!" he yelled at Lora. "I don't want to hear any more!"

Lora switched it off as Alex, his face flushed, stood by the window. The room fell silent for a moment as he regained his composure.

"So here at the Academy you want to help us, to teach us," Sam said. Then he asked in a steely voice, "What does the Enterprise want with us?"

"Their primary goal is to understand what makes you so . . . special," the Professor answered. "Their approach is different from the Academy's. While we teach and guide, they design and push. Your true dreams, your nightmares, may seem to occur naturally, but in fact it is planned from the very start of your lives. They made you that way."

"True dreams mean seeing the future?" Sam asked.

The Professor nodded. "As you know, Eva has already had a dream that turned out to be an exact prediction of the future," he continued. "Here, we teach our students to develop these skills and learn how to use that foresight to affect what will come to pass in real life. We can guide you so that instead of having only a glimpse of the future, past or present, you can expand your dreams and even share them with other Dreamers."

Alex let out a snort. "Oh man, that's rich." He paced

behind his chair, facing the Professor and Lora. "*Seeing* the future? Yeah, right. Seriously, you guys are full of it! Crackpots, feeding us a pack of lies."

"All right," the Professor said. "What if I told you that among what we teach here is how to control your dreams to *change* the future? The real, living, waking future."

"How can we possibly believe that?" Alex went on. "This is some kind of con, a trick—you're running some kind of weird cult up here in the mountains! You've *kidnapped* us, and I want to be taken—"

"To the nearest embassy?" the Professor said. "To the police?"

Alex remained silent.

"Come on, guys," Alex looked at Eva and then Sam, "let's get out of here."

"We'll take you anywhere you want to go," Lora said, "Anywhere at all."

"Yet," Alex replied, "I sense a big hairy *but* around the corner."

Lora laughed, and said, "We *will* take you anywhere. The 'but,' if there's one, is that all we ask, all *I* ask, is that you hear us out."

"I think we've heard enough," Alex said. "Guys?"

"Alex," Eva said. "What about my dream about meeting the two of you? That came true."

"So?" Alex said.

"And the helicopter—"

"Fine, Eva, you stay here with these crazies," he said. "Sam?"

"What about *my* dream?" Sam said. He saw Lora's face change when he said that, as if she was remembering the details of what he'd told her at the subway. "What if *that* becomes real?"

"Sam, come on man!" Alex continued to pace. "Dreams coming true? Maybe there have been some coincidences, but you can't seriously believe this! This is garbage!" He looked at the Professor, expecting an explanation.

The Professor let out a sigh. "I know this is a lot to process, and I am sorry for that. But I'm afraid there is no time to waste."

The three teens listened intently.

"From the moment you dreamed last night, Sam, something started," the Professor said. "There is a battle coming. Time is against us now. Sam, your dream shows that you will be among a small group of true Dreamers, thirteen in all, that represent our last hope for the future. Maybe Eva and Alex will be too."

Sam shifted uneasily in his seat. *Maybe all three of us? So why did the Enterprise pick Alex up? Did he dream something that he doesn't want us to know about? Could anything be worse than my dream?*

"You guys can talk all you want," Alex said. "I want to see proof."

"Well, it's all about *mind over matter*," the Professor said, and Sam noticed Lora smiling at the obviously familiar rhetoric. "Through study, we are learning to tap into more of our minds."

"Or to put it another way," Lora added, "schooling and experience expands the mind and teaches you how to use it. Studies have shown that people only use a fraction of their brains at any given time. Well, at the Academy, we provide our students—selected by the world's top scholars—with the focus and skills to go one step further. Our work here, beyond a usual school curriculum, is to guide students to develop a greater part of their brain function, accessed via their dreams, which in turn leads to far higher learning abilities."

"What for?" Sam asked.

"So that the world gets its next da Vincis and Einsteins," the Professor added. "And also, so that we are better prepared for the race ahead."

"What is this race?" Sam asked. "I mean, once all of the last 13 are found, these thirteen true Dreamers, then what?"

"You make it sound simple, Sam, but finding the last 13 will prove very difficult," the Professor said. "We have been waiting centuries for this race to even begin. The lore says that once the Dreamers are found, then the fate of the world is . . ." He paused, composing his thoughts. "The 'race' is the last battle for the ultimate power in the world."

"Ultimate power?" Sam said.

The Professor nodded. "The 13 Dreamers who we hope to find in the coming weeks are the last group on earth who can save us all."

"Right, so now you're suggesting we're in some kind of final war? For the whole world?" Alex laughed and shook his head. "What do you take us for? I want proof or I'm leaving."

"I think I might have it," Sam said, anxiously. "I think I saw the proof, in my dream."

17

"Sam, can you tell us about the dream you had last night?" the Professor asked.

Sam recounted his dream and this time he didn't hold anything back. At the end he looked at Lora and said, "You were there, with me."

Lora's face showed a confusion of emotions but she remained controlled. "I suspected something like that when you first looked at me today. You recognized me."

Sam nodded. Eva sat still, wide-eyed. Now even Alex was silent.

"Sam, could you try drawing the crystal from your dream?" the Professor asked.

Sam took the offered pad and pencil, but when he tried to focus on his memory of the object, it was clouded; he just couldn't remember. His thoughts took him back to the moment when he looked down at his opened hand but he was immediately distracted by the flash of light—the horror of that deadly moment.

"Argh!" Sam said, looking away, spooked. He knew it was no good. He just couldn't get a clear image of the crystal in his mind. He looked at the expectant faces of Lora, Alex, Eva and the Professor. "I'm sorry, I can't."

"That's OK," Lora said. "It takes practice to recall dreams."

"I—I saw it, a glimpse, but then . . ." Sam struggled to put it into words.

"I don't get it. What's so special about this object?" Alex asked.

"I'm not sure . . ." the Professor said, looking genuinely lost in thought. "But it does seem to be the key to Sam's whole dream, especially as *he* wants it."

"And what about this prophecy that gets mentioned? What does it say, do you know?" Eva asked.

"Oh yes, we know the prophecy well," the Professor said. He tapped on a computer screen and brought up an image. "This text has been translated from an ancient form of Egyptian. It was found on one half of a tablet, belonging to Ramses II. The tablet was broken, and the second half has never been found."

"Never been found?" Eva said. "So all of this you've said about a battle and our supposed destiny is based on only half a prophecy?"

The Professor looked at Eva's concerned face. "Half a prophecy perhaps, but also centuries of the greatest true Dreamers' predictions and concentrated historical and archaeological study. This prophecy is just one piece of the puzzle."

They inched closer to the screen for a better look.
Sam read the words aloud—

Dreaming of their destiny,
Minds entwined, thirteen will be.
Falter not, the last cannot fall,
Or Solaris shall rule over all.

"Wow, that doesn't sound serious at all," Alex said. "I mean like, no pressure, right?"

"You can say that again," Sam said. He suddenly felt pale and tired. "Solaris? Is that something to do with the sun?"

Just then, a bell rang out.

"What's that?" Alex asked, Sam's question forgotten for the moment.

"Dinner," Lora said. "Ten minute call."

The door to the office opened and the secretary entered, pointed to her watch and said, "Professor, the helicopter is ready for you."

"Yes, thank you, I'll be there in a moment." The Professor turned back to them. "We will continue this conversation later. I must go to a crisis meeting in Paris, but I will return as soon as possible." He held up his hand as Alex began to protest. "I know you have even more questions for me now. But Lora and Sebastian will give you as many answers as they can until then."

The group reluctantly stood up, and made for the door.

"Hate to rain on your parade, Professor, sir," Alex said. "But I haven't dreamed of any prophecy or anything like that. I never even remember my dreams."

The Professor turned and said, "Never? Really?"

Alex shook his head.

"Not even a nightmare, perhaps?"

Sam could see a nervous twitch in Alex's face.

"Say I'm starting to believe you . . ." Alex said. "Do you really think that we—that Sam, at least, is part of this last 13?"

"I don't think it," the Professor said, smiling as he wrapped a scarf around his neck to head outside. "I know it."

18

Sam followed the others in a daze.

Lora led the way towards the dining hall. But Sam wasn't hungry. He couldn't imagine trying to eat right now. *Who were the last 13? How was it he was supposedly one of these people who years—centuries—later would fulfill some prophecy about the fate of the world?*

"I'll take you via the dorms," Lora said, then paused and looked at them all. "Could I ask you all not to tell other students here details about your dreams, not yet—it might create panic. We'll handle it after we've dealt with Sam's dream."

"After we've dealt with it?" Sam said, feeling ill.

"The shadowy figure you described," Lora said, "is known as Solaris, an evil force that will face the last 13 in the battle. Having a *true dream* of Solaris has long been regarded as a sign of being one of the last 13, as is dreaming of the prophecy itself. We have the technology here whereby you can reenter your dream, play it out from start to finish. We need to get you over to the labs tomorrow. The more we know, the better prepared we can be."

Sam recalled that Lora was there with him in his nightmare and how there'd been the flash of light and then nothing. *Now they want me to reenter it—relive it all again? Face that thing, who is probably this Solaris, and maybe see it through even further, to its grisly conclusion . . .*

"Lora, in my dream, the figure, Solaris, clicked his fingers and killed everyone in the entire city with fire. Could that really come true?"

"I hope not, Sam. Dreams have a habit of getting pretty unreal if you don't know how to control them, even true dreams. Especially if some part of it features something you're afraid of. Like fire, for example."

Sam looked at Lora. He needed some space to think.

"Can you give us five?" he asked Lora. "Alone?"

"Sure. This is your room for the night, anyway. Eva's is four doors down. Just follow the other students from here to the dining hall when you're ready. I'll see you all a bit later."

Sam watched her walk away.

As soon as they were alone, Alex whistled.

"Makes you wonder, doesn't it? I mean, why isn't it some genius, or super-strong guy . . . or girl," Alex said. "Or a Nobel laureate, or an Olympian or something."

"Huh?" Sam said.

"I'm just saying—why *you*?" Alex asked.

"Why me what?" Sam said.

"You know, saving the world and all that. Shouldn't it be

someone more, well, qualified? A hero, a soldier—even a president or something."

"What about teens in movies?" Sam said. "They're always a nobody and they manage to save the world."

"Yeah," Alex said, "with spy gadgets or superheroes or robots helping them, no doubt."

"Well, we've got a prophecy. And according to that, there's another twelve true Dreamers still to come."

"Yeah, well, I don't see any caped crusaders or robots helping you out, that's all I'm saying."

"Would you guys stop it!" Eva said. "This is serious!"

"Geez, I dunno," Sam mumbled. "Anyway, a few minutes ago it sounded like *you* thought this was all made up?"

Alex leaned against the hallway wall.

"Look, you heard them back there," Alex said, tugging at his T-shirt collar as though it was stifling him. "What they said about dreaming real things and learning how to better control your mind."

"So you're saying that you believe them now?" Eva said. "All this dreaming stuff?"

"Let's say that I'm starting to believe."

"Right," Sam said, uncomfortable, wanting to distract them. He opened the door.

They all stopped talking at the sight of the room before them.

There was a bed on each side with a window in the middle, pretty standard dorm arrangements. But it was the wall-to-wall shelves that impressed the two boys—there was every gizmo imaginable and then some.

"This is . . ." Alex said.

". . . amazing," Sam finished.

"Tell me I'm not dreaming."

Sam punched Alex in the arm.

"Ouch. Thanks. OK, this is awesome."

"I'll leave you boys to it," Eva said and headed down the hall to her room.

Sam sat on his bed. Every little detail was how he'd imagined a dream bedroom to be: there were a couple of beanbags before a massive screen on one wall set up with games consoles, tablets, books, everything.

"Isn't this the coolest bedroom you've ever seen?" Alex said, checking out the bounty on his shelves and bedside table. "It's like everything I would ever want or need is here—a home away from home stuffed into a mountain-top castle and injected with cash."

"Yeah," Sam agreed, lost in the wonder of it all. *This morning I woke in a sweat from a nightmare, and after all that's happened today . . . and being told that I have to save the world, now I'm here. I couldn't have imagined any of this in my wildest dreams.*

19

Sam and Alex were late. They joined Eva at a table in the dining hall across from a black-haired kid with the world's thickest eyebrows growing over red-rimmed glasses. He looked no more than thirteen years old. He stared at Sam. The whole room stared at Sam—hundreds of pairs of eyes. Even the teaching staff were watching him. Slowly the hum of conversation resumed. It looked like word had gotten around, despite Lora's warning, about Sam and his connection to the legendary prophecy.

"You're him, aren't you?" Eyebrows asked. He bit nervously at his bottom lip.

"Not really sure who *him* is," Sam said, looking at big platters of food spread down the middle of the table. He loaded up his plate with steak, fries and salad.

"The first Dreamer," the boy said. "I mean, they say you're one of the—one of the last 13!"

"Yeah, it's something like that," Alex said through a mouthful of food. "I'm Alex, and this is Sam and Eva."

"Everyone here calls me Pi," the boy said, fidgeting in his seat and looking at the other students at their table, all of them eating quietly while continuing to steal glances at Sam. "Sam, it's really an honor to meet you. Have you . . . have you had your first dream?"

Sam nodded and put down his cutlery, looking at the grill marks on the meat, his appetite gone.

"Not hungry? Want some of my nachos?" Eva asked.

Sam shook his head, thinking about his nightmare and the flash and the falling ash. *Hardly something to be jealous of, if you ask me.*

"He'll eat," Alex said, his mouth full. "Eva, is your room as awesome as ours?"

"It's even better!" Eva said, launching into a description of how it was everything she'd ever wanted.

Pi watched Sam, until finally Sam stopped staring at the table.

"What happens after this?" Sam asked him.

Pi was quiet for a moment, as if pondering the possible answers, and then said, "Dessert?"

Sam laughed. "No, Pi, I mean, in general. Like those uniformed guys—what are they supposed to be guarding us against? I mean, we're all the way up here in the mountains." Sam motioned to a few guards with the same horse insignia on their lapels their driver had worn. There were maybe a dozen of them, standing at the edges of the room.

"Do they protect us from the Enterprise?" Eva said.

"Yes, but from what I hear, the Enterprise are nothing compared to the real bad guys," Pi said. "I mean, so I'm told. And they're new to the scene, the Enterprise that is, they're 20th century. Not worth worrying about, with our Guardians around."

"Guardians don't look so tough," Alex said.

"They're kinda like the Swiss Guards, but our Guardians are bigger, faster and stronger than the best of them. These Guardians would eat most security guys for breakfast," Pi chuckled awkwardly.

"Pi, who are the real bad guys?" Eva asked.

"You mean Solaris, right?" Sam added.

Pi leaned forward and whispered: "Solaris is . . ."

The doors burst open and a platoon of big, solid-looking men took up standing positions just inside the room.

Alex said, "More Guardians?"

"Maybe they heard you say they weren't that tough," Sam said.

"What's going on?" Eva asked Pi, as the awed silence of the room broke and whispers fanned out as quickly as the armed guys had.

"Security is being beefed up," Pi said.

Sam looked at Pi, curious if the boy was making a joke, but he seemed serious, worried even.

"Why would they do that?" Sam asked.

"Maybe they received a threat against this place," Pi said. "Perhaps an alarm got triggered—it's happened before, like when there's an avalanche on the mountain and it knocks out the main power, or trips one of the security sensors. Or it could be . . ."

There were tense conversations at all the tables.

"What?" Eva asked.

"Must have been a threat against the Academy," Pi said, clearly backtracking on what he was going to say.

"Or what, Pi?" Eva asked. "What else?"

By the guilty look he gave Sam, Sam understood what Pi meant and his stomach dropped.

"I get it," Sam said, noticing that the teachers were all looking over at him. "They're here because I'm here. My dream last night has started this race. Everyone here is in danger because of me."

20

The students were ushered to the dormitory wing, up above the main living level. Many congregated in a few rooms, talking in whispers, the buzz palpable. If there was a lights-out curfew, Sam had not heard about it. He was glad to be out of the dining hall, where the students had vied for Sam's attention. He'd felt like a caged animal, with everyone gawking, as he was the only one so far identified as a genuine contender in the race.

"Why would they want this?" Sam asked Pi, sitting on the floor of the boys' bedroom, along with Alex and Eva. "What I have, I mean. The dream. The attention. The danger."

"Sam, this is a dream come true for many of them," Pi answered.

"Ha!" Alex said. "Well, I've yet to see a dream of mine come true—for instance, where's my gold-plated hover-craft, my supermodel girlfriend and my private island?"

"I thought you couldn't remember your dreams," Sam said jokingly.

"Well, I can daydream, can't I?" Alex replied and gave

him a playful punch in the arm.

"But Sam's right about the danger," Eva said, ignoring the boys' antics. "From what we've heard, there's every chance people might get *killed*."

A group of girls ran by the doorway, giggling as they stole glances at Sam.

"Pi, they've brought in the German Guards!" a blond-haired boy shouted into their room, then he saw Sam and bolted from view.

"What does that mean?" Eva asked Pi.

"The Guardians from Germany must be here," Pi said. "I think there are about fifty of them, and they're considered to be the best of all the Guardians."

He looked distant.

"What is it?" Sam asked.

"It means they must have closed the German safe houses," Pi said. "Sent everyone to France or Italy, or the Netherlands—the other continental bases. Poland is just a skeleton camp anyway, like Spain, Austria and Denmark . . . no one's there permanently. Greece closed ages back."

"So there are even more guards here now?" Alex asked.

"Yeah."

"There were like a hundred or so before."

"Their training camp, in Morocco, sent their whole contingent of new graduates here earlier today," Pi said. "I guess that was when word first came that you were arriving. I wonder if the Professor foresaw it."

"You sure know a lot about all these guard movements," Alex said.

"My brother's a Guardian in London," Pi said. "He missed out on being a Dreamer, but he has other skills."

"He's built like a wrestler?" Alex said.

"Something like that," Pi said, with a shy smile. "He's way bigger than me."

"Surely we're safe up here in the mountains?" Eva asked. "It's so remote."

"Maybe," Pi said with a shrug. "But if Sam is here, and if he really is the first Dreamer in the prophecy, then it means the race has finally begun."

"And that no one is safe," Eva added.

Sam swallowed hard. He understood what that meant for him—that he would have to live out his nightmare by confronting the figure he now knew as Solaris, the so-called "ultimate evil," who hides in the darkest shadows, stalking him. *When that time comes, will I have Guardians with me? Will my friends—if that's what they are—be there?* He looked at Eva, Alex and Pi. *Will they be there, or will it be just me and Lora?*

There was commotion in the hallway and a few students sprinted by.

"Everyone to their own rooms, right now!" they heard Sebastian say gruffly, then he appeared in the doorway, his shadow cast over them from where he stood in the brightly lit corridor. "You all need your rest. Sam, you especially."

Then Sebastian was gone as quickly as he'd appeared.

"I don't like him," Eva whispered to them as she prepared to leave.

"Well, get used to him because he'll be playing a big part in this," Pi said. "He's the Professor's son."

"Him? You wouldn't know it," Eva replied. "I mean, you'd hardly say they were alike."

"He's tough but fair. You just have to get used to his moods," Pi said. "He's a great teacher—super-smart, very good at what he does."

"Giving me the heebie-jeebies?" Alex said. "Yeah, he's good at that."

"You asleep?" Alex asked in their dark bedroom.

"Yeah, doofus, I'm sound asleep," Sam said. He was reading through the Academy's history on an electronic tablet. Sam was in no hurry to get to sleep—*who knows what nightmares I might have next. Maybe I'll just stay awake forever.* "And right now I'm having a dream where you're a different version of you—one who doesn't snore."

"Ha, like I was snoring!"

"You were five minutes ago."

"That was a snort," Alex retorted. "A schnort. Called it! Whole new word, invented on the spot. Anyway, whatcha reading?"

"Right now, prophecy-type stuff. You?"

Alex flipped around his screen, showing notes from an Academy computer class. "Computers are my thing—but I gotta say, they never taught us *this* level of programming at regular school. I mean, this is fierce. How about you—you learned anything useful?"

"Yeah and no," Sam said, scrolling through the pages. "I've learned that whatever's coming, if all these theories are correct . . . let's just say I've got a real time ahead of me."

"We, buddy," Alex said. "It's not all about you, remember?"

"Yeah, well . . ." Sam put the tablet aside. "So, want to talk about whatever your dream was that got you here?"

"Not really, no," Alex said. "You want to talk about why you flipped out in the aura corridor?"

"Not really, no," Sam said. *Maybe another time.*

There was a faint knock at their door. It opened a little and Sam watched a figure enter the darkness and the door closed again.

"Eva?" Sam said, straining to see, the room lit only by his tablet's screen.

"Yep," she replied, emerging from the gloom and sitting on the end of Sam's bed.

"Couldn't sleep," she said.

Alex *schnorted* and said, "So Dream Girl thought she'd come and hassle Dream Boy here?"

Sam threw a pillow at him in reply.

"What if we *were* asleep?"

"As if," Eva said, standing up and taking the discarded pillow to use as a cushion on the floor between the boys.

"I—I can't stop thinking about my parents," Eva said. "Who they *really* are, I mean."

"Me too," Sam said.

"Trust me, we'll get answers," Alex said. "And soon, don't you worry. I'm making a list."

"List?" Sam said.

"Two, actually," Alex replied. "One full of the questions I want answered, and another with the people here I don't like or trust—which is pretty much the whole teaching staff so far."

Eva laughed. "You idiot."

"What?"

"Just because you don't know them—"

"Hey, it's my opinion, OK?" He chuckled and said, "Don't make me add you to the list."

"I'm fine with that," Eva said, making a face at him. "Maybe I've got a list of my own: you!"

Sam could see the two of them were trying to ease the tension, but it made him think: *how can any of us trust each other, really trust, with everything that is happening?* It would have to be enough that for now, they were all in the same boat. *But how long will that last?*

"So, what else?" Sam asked. "Something's up, right?"

Eva was silent a moment and then admitted, "I want to go see those paintings again."

"Why?" Sam said.

"I read about them," Eva said, "in a book about the Academy's history—"

"Which volume?" Sam asked.

"One," Eva replied. "1493–1543. I thought I should start

at the beginning."

"Ah, I'm flicking through volume eleven," Sam replied. "1943–1993."

"You guys are history geeks," Alex said. "Great. You've both just made my list."

"So what about the paintings?" Sam said, ignoring Alex's wisecracks and at the same time getting a nervous sensation at the thought of walking back through that corridor again.

"So what? They're fascinating," Eva said. "They show important Dreamers, some who've been famous geniuses, others not so well known, or even just seemingly your average Joe. And they were made of all those tiny pictures, the gears and stuff."

"And . . ." Alex said. "Lame much?"

"You're lame!" Eva said, tossing the pillow back. "And as if you guys can sleep! Come on, I know you're as curious about this place as I am, so let's go exploring."

"We've got everything we need here," Sam said.

"Everything but answers."

"We've got, like, about every book in the world on these computers," Sam said.

"Just a little look . . ."

Alex relented. "I'm in," he said, getting out of bed to reveal he was still wearing his clothes. "I was gonna have a creep around tonight anyway, see what else I could find out."

"Cool. Sam?"

"No."

"Come on . . ."

Sam smiled and threw back his sheet. He was still dressed too.

"I was thinking about sneaking around too," he said, grinning. "Let's go. We'll see how far we get before those über-Guardians catch us!"

Sam stood next to Eva and Alex, the three of them looking at the large collage portraits. Even by the dim illumination of the tiny night-lights, they could make out the collage of tiny individual faces and mechanical gears that made up the image of the dominant portrait.

"What was that?" Eva whispered.

"What was what?" Alex said.

"I heard a noise."

"It's nothing."

"Maybe it's something."

"Maybe it's some *thing* . . ."

"That's not funny."

"Maybe they have killer guard dogs from another dimension."

"Maybe it's the Professor's dogs," Sam said, trying to calm them down. He looked around. The place was smothered in dark shadows. Eva nudged in a bit closer behind him.

"There's nobody here," Alex said, peering around the hall.

"Let's head back," Eva said.

"We just got here."

"I've had enough, let's go."

"Chicken."

"I'm going," Eva said—and let out a stifled shriek as she collided into something. Sam took his hand from her mouth—she'd bumped into him.

"It's probably just those guards doing a security sweep," he whispered. "Come on, follow me."

"**G**reat," Eva said. "Now we're lost."

Sam looked back the way that they'd come. They'd taken a couple of wrong turns somewhere, and with the halls in near-darkness, it was hard to make out anywhere that looked vaguely familiar.

"Nice one, fearless leader," Eva said.

"Well, it is kind of dark," Alex said, sheepishly giving up the position up front.

"Shh!" Sam said, pausing at a set of double doors. "Listen."

There was a scraping noise, and then nothing.

"Let's check it out," Sam whispered. He put his hand on the doorknob.

"What are you doing?" Eva whispered.

"Just checking it out . . ." Sam stopped, closed an eye and peered with the other through the gap between the doors. "Can't see anything . . . it's too dark."

"That's it, I'm going in," Alex said, and pushed open the door.

The three of them cautiously tiptoed into the dark room

and held their breath, listening for another movement. Sam moved further forward, towards the moonlit window opposite the door. The faint light shining through it was just enough to turn every shadow in the room into a sinister shape. He slowly advanced, Eva and Alex keeping still and watchful behind him. Sam reached the window, and felt a breeze.

It was open slightly.

His feet squelched on the carpet.

The floor was wet, and crunched slightly with a little snow that had yet to melt.

"Hey, guys," he whispered, "I think someone climbed in through the . . ."

"Sam!" Eva cried, then clutched her hands over her mouth.

A tall figure stood behind Sam.

Sam turned around, a cold shiver running up and down his spine. *If this is it, if this is Solaris, I hope he makes it quick. I don't want to see him burn everyone . . .*

"Students here should know how dangerous it is to be out of their rooms at night," the tall figure's voice said. "Especially when the place is overrun by Guardians. Do you really want to bump into *them* in the dark? All kinds of accidents could happen. Turn on the light, it's by the door."

Sam heard Alex move to the light switch.

"Hello, Sam."

As light filled the room, Sam turned around at the voice, which he now recognized.

"Mr. Cole?"

Sam's high school science teacher smiled and said, "Good to see you."

"But . . ." Sam said, "what are *you* doing here?"

"Please, call me Tobias."

"Hang on, *Tobias*," Alex interrupted. "Sam, what's going on? Who is this old dude?"

"This is Mr. Cole—Tobias Cole—my science teacher," Sam said, bewildered.

"And he's just made my list for nearly making me pee my pants," Alex said, sitting in an armchair and letting out a sigh.

Sam looked at his teacher and said, "How . . . I mean, why . . ."

"Well, I'm surprised it isn't obvious," Mr. Cole said to Sam.

"Obvious?" Sam said.

"I work for the Academy, Sam," Tobias said, sitting on a stool and easing off his gloves. "My assignment for the last few years has been to watch over you. Making sure you were OK. Making sure that if you ended up being a Dreamer, like we thought you might, you'd be ready for true dreaming. I saw to it that you learned as much as I could teach you—without raising any suspicions—and to help keep you safe."

Sam went to say something but his mind failed him, his mouth moving but nothing coming out.

"As for the window here . . . it's a worry," Tobias said, checking the wet carpet by their feet, little specks of white snow twinkling against the light. "This is a teachers' work room. I came in to put my things down. I was just going to dump my papers on the desk, so I didn't bother to turn on the light, but now I've seen this open window."

"Someone snuck in?" Sam said.

"Perhaps. Could be a student, it's happened often enough, even when I went to school here. We used to hike out to one of the caves which we stocked with snack foods and tell scary stories. Someone has probably just been careless and forgotten to close it. But it could be something more sinister, which is why you should not leave your rooms at night."

"We should tell the Guardians," Eva said.

"I'll mention it," Tobias replied. "Let's hope there's nothing to worry about. There's two squads of Guardians outside doing a sweep of the mountain, and others wandering the corridors. Really, I'm surprised the three of you didn't get darted."

"As if we'd let someone dart us," Alex said, smiling, then he added, "again."

"So . . ." Sam said to Tobias, "you're *not* a normal teacher?"

"Sam, you've been learning more about this true dreaming business than you might imagine," Tobias said with a smile. "Quite a few deviations from the curriculum, but all for the better, I assure you. Humph, they should teach my classes worldwide if you ask me."

"Why didn't you ever say anything?"

He shook his head and said, "It had to be that way. Still, it all seemed to work out, right? You're here now. Who are your friends?"

"Oh, they're not . . . I mean, they're . . ."

"He's trying to say that we just met," Eva said. "I'm Eva, and this is Alex."

"Tobias Cole, the third," the teacher said in introduction.

Eva seemed to come alive. "I recognize that name," she said. "Are you related to the Tobias Cole I saw in the portrait gallery?"

"Yes," he replied. "My grandfather. Quite a Dreamer he was. I never amounted to much more than being able to teach."

"What do you teach?" Eva asked.

"I designed a lot of the courses actually—Noetics is my baby."

"No—what?"

"Essentially, the way we teach it here, it's dream manipulation, control," he said. "I guess you probably all need to work on your dreaming a bit more. On remembering, controlling the information you get within the dream. Also in learning how to stop it from going into the dark places in your imagination. You might notice dreams, even true dreams, have a nasty habit of picking up on what you're most afraid of."

Sam thought about the fire.

"Don't worry," Tobias said. "It takes practice, and I'm here to help."

"I don't think I really want to work on dreaming," Sam said. "According to my dream, terrible things are going to happen."

"You'll be fine, Sam," Tobias said. "You'll see. The reality is never as bad as the nightmare itself."

"What do you mean?"

"Well, we can dream anything our imagination allows, right? But reality is bound by rules—the laws of physics, for example. You might fly in a dream, even in a 'true' dream, but that doesn't mean you're about to sprout wings. The trick is remembering what's real and what's just the dream. And the longer you true dream, the more blurred the lines become."

"I'm not sure all of this makes sense yet," Sam said.

"Understanding will come with experience. But just to be safe, I'd like you all to wear these." Tobias handed the trio necklaces that were made of a simple loop of leather, on which hung a small, woven dream catcher charm, each with its own unique design.

"They're beautiful!" Eva said.

"Cool!" said Alex.

"What are these for?" asked Sam.

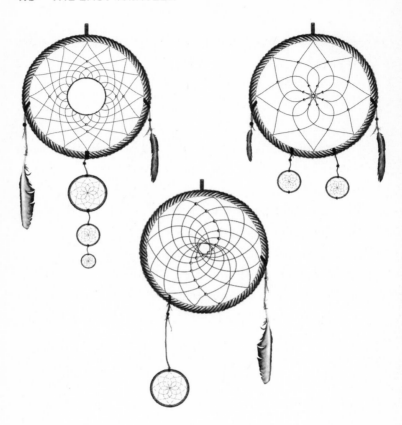

"Some would say they're just a little Dreamer super-stition," Tobias said, "to keep your mind balanced and help stop your true dreams from being too influenced by your imagination."

"You mean it'll keep nightmares away?" Alex asked.

"Some nightmares, sure," Tobias said. "Once you put it on, try not to take it off. It's also a symbol of protection. Superstitious maybe, but we all wear them. It's one way to tell an Academy graduate out in the real world. You've probably seen the emblems on the uniforms here too."

"Yeah. OK," Alex said. "Thanks."

Tobias looked towards the door, and frowned. "Ah, Seb. It's been a while. Would you like to join us?"

Sam turned around. Sebastian stood by the door—he'd entered the room as quietly as a ghost.

"Tobias," he said. "I see you're back."

"I'm needed," Tobias replied.

"Really?"

"Oh yes, the race has begun," Tobias said. "Or didn't you hear?"

"So some believe," Sebastian said.

"And you don't?" Tobias asked in surprise.

"I've seen a few false alarms over the years, so I'm yet to be convinced by these . . ." Sebastian looked at the three teens, "kids."

Tobias looked at Sebastian. Sam sensed there was definitely some friction between these two men.

"They shouldn't be out of their dorms," Sebastian added.

"We're not in a prison," Alex said.

"No, I guess not," Sebastian said. "It's for your safety though—our mountain surveillance crew just found evidence that someone has been looking around outside." He looked at Tobias meaningfully, then turned to Sam and the others. "Back to your rooms, now—if we know where you are, we can better protect you."

Sam said goodbye to Tobias and led Eva and Alex back to their dorms, following the directions Sebastian had just given them. The encounter with Tobias and Sebastian left him feeling uneasy, confused and even more worried. But seeing his teacher, knowing he was there, gave him hope.

23

After a restless night—during which none of them seemed to have slept very much, let alone dreamed—Sam, Eva and Alex braved the dining hall once more. Sparkling sunlight poured in through the high windows, giving the room a warm glow. Sam was pleased to see lots of smiling faces around, and it felt as though dread and worry didn't last long in this place.

"You guys sleep all right?" Alex asked as they lined up for breakfast.

Sam and Eva shrugged.

"Dream?"

They shook their heads.

"Yeah, same here," Alex said, then started attacking his stack of pancakes as they walked to a table.

"I miss my mom. Is that weird?" Eva said quietly. "I mean, I know she's not really my mom, but . . ." They were each trying not to make eye contact with the dozens of students still staring at them.

Sam patted her shoulder. "It's OK, I know what you mean. I miss my dopey little brother." *And that's not all*, Sam thought, imagining Scout's happy face, and his parents' caring concern. He even missed the morning ritual of sleeping through his alarm and his mom shouting the house down to wake him up and get him to school on time.

They found a space on one of the long tables as Pi waved from across the room. Opposite them, two students smiled in greeting.

"Hi, Sam," the girl with long blond hair said shyly. "It is Sam, isn't it?"

"Yes, that's me. Eva and Alex," Sam said, gesturing to the others.

"Nice to finally meet you. I'm Charlotte, and this is . . ."

"Oscar—awesome to meet you guys!" the boy said. His bright-red hair bobbed as he spoke enthusiastically, reaching out to shake Sam's hand. "How are you settling in? Managed to avoid Seb so far and hang out with Lora? She's cool, isn't she?"

"She seems great, I guess . . ." Sam started.

"Watch out, he's testing you," Charlotte warned. "Lora's his big sister."

"Well, in that case, she's definitely great." Sam grinned. "You been living here for long?"

"Oscar's whole family are practically part of the Academy, so he's always been around. I've only been here for six months so far, but I'm loving it." Charlotte's give-away smile to Oscar made it clear they were close friends already.

"Maybe we can pick up a few tips from you while we're here, then," Eva said.

"As it happens, Char and I have been chosen to show you the ropes while Sam is at the lab, so it's your lucky day!" Oscar grinned broadly. "We're meeting in the room at the end of this corridor," Oscar pointed behind him, "in about half an hour, so you've got enough time to enjoy your pancakes." Oscar raised his eyebrows at Alex, who paused midway between shoveling forkfuls of breakfast into his waiting mouth.

"What?"

24

The Professor had returned to the Academy and Sam was anxious to see him. He didn't have to wait long.

"Sam, how are you settling in?" the Professor asked as they walked along a long corridor that sloped below the dining hall, and seemed to be cut into the solid rock of the granite mountain. It was colder than the levels above and lit by banks of lights throwing stark bright light and deep black shadows.

"I'm settling in OK I guess," Sam said. "Met some students, got shown around . . . I guess it's hard to know what I *think* right now. It's a lot to take in. How was your meeting in Paris?"

"The Dreamer Council are interested in your arrival, to say the least, and will assist you in any way possible," the Professor said.

"Me?"

"Our world has been waiting a long time for this day to come, so I'm sure you can appreciate that you're big news. I told the Council that we need more information from your dream first before anything else can happen."

Sam's mind was racing at a million miles an hour. *All these people really think that I'm some prophesized Dreamer?*

"Why is it me?" Sam asked, as they descended a spiral staircase cut into the stone. "I don't see why I'm any different from anyone else. There's nothing special about me."

"And yet, there must be. Take heart, you will not be on this journey alone. For now, we need to know what our next step will be. We're going to reenter your last dream," the Professor said. "We'll go to the very core of it, mine every detail. We'll soon know for sure if it is a true dream or not."

Sam's heart sank.

"Here we are," the Professor said. There were two doors at the end of the long twisting corridor and the Professor turned the handle on the door to the right. It opened with a hermetically sealed *hiss* and even colder air spewed out. Sam couldn't help but wonder what was behind the door on the left.

The Professor led Sam into a room with round glass walls, which looked down over another sunken level full of tall banks of computer towers, crisscrossed with cables and cooling tubes. "This," the Professor said, "is the nerve center of the Academy—our computing hub. We're in the levels below the hangar now."

They entered a sealed-off glass room where it was warm again, and where a man turned around in a swivel chair. Sam had seen him before, sitting at the teachers' table in the dining hall, so he must have been faculty staff. But he was young for a staff member, no more than eighteen.

"And this here is Dr. Joe Jedko," the Professor said, "our computer genius."

"They call me JJ, or Dr. J, though I wish they'd call me Jedi," he said with a big grin. He was dressed in a Hawaiian shirt and board shorts, and had the pale skin of some of the computer geeks Sam knew at high school—the kind of complexion that didn't see the light of day—only the glow of computer screens. "Sam, right?"

"Nice to meet you, Jedi," Sam said, shaking his hand. He seemed to be pleased that Sam took straight to calling him that. "This is a cool setup."

Sam stood at the glass window, looking out at the room full of computing power below. Aside from the tall banks of black computer towers, there was a section with shelf upon shelf of—

"Are they . . ." Sam pressed his nose to the glass to see in greater detail. "Are they gaming consoles?"

"You know it," Jedi said. "I've got a cluster of over two thousand of them running to form a supercomputer."

"No way!"

"Way," he replied. "The console cluster, when connected to all the others around the world online at any given moment, gives me some decent exaflops of power—near on infinite computability."

"Whatever that was you just said," Sam said, "it sounds way cool."

Jedi smiled and gave two thumbs-up.

"Oh, hey," Sam said, producing his waterlogged phone, wrecked from its dramatic plunge into the backyard pool. "Any chance you can make me a phone that doesn't get so easily trashed?"

"You should have invested in a five dollar cover," Jedi said, inspecting the visible damage.

"I think I'm going to need something a little more, you know, military-spec," Sam said, "that can stand up to getting knocked around."

"Hmm, I can try," he said. "Maybe an armored outer shell . . ."

Sam shrugged and the Professor smiled. There was a sound at the door, and Lora walked into the room.

"Leave it with me," Jedi said with a grin. "So, Professor, into the Dream Machine?"

"Yes, thank you, Dr. J," the Professor said, "but it will be Lora guiding Sam through this dream. I'll watch on the monitor. Lora?"

"Yes, I'm ready," Lora said. "Sam, as I was present in your original dream, then I will be able to help you more easily now."

Sam nodded, happy to see her there to guide him, though he couldn't help feeling that she looked a little uneasy at the prospect.

The four of them moved to an area of the room where there were two reclining armchairs set up side by side.

Lora sat in one and Jedi guided Sam to the other. What looked like motorcycle helmets were put on their heads, with wires linking them to a shared console in between. "Sam, this device will allow us to reenter your most recent dream and record the details."

"Record?" Sam said.

"The beauty of this Dream Machine is the computer-mind interface program I designed," Jedi said. "We can record the playback of your dream, right down to the smallest details—things you can't recall, things you probably didn't even notice when you were in there."

"And remember, this time we will take your dream further, from its natural beginning to its natural end point," the Professor said. Lora pulled her visor down and Sam did the same. Immediately he saw that there was a display on the inside of the visor—computer code whirled down the screen, then the image changed to a night sky and he felt as if he were flying through clouds and looking around at stars and a pale moon.

Sam swallowed hard and signaled with a thumbs-up that he was ready. It felt warm all of a sudden, and he realized the chair had little vents in it, blowing heated air around him.

"Just relax," Lora said.

"OK, lean back and enjoy the ride." Jedi grinned, his finger paused over the ENTER key, ready to run the program. Sam lay back and focused on the images of the balmy night sky. "And don't worry, you won't feel a thing."

I sit at a table in a crowded cafe. It feels like I've been here before. I turn to my reflection in the window and see that I look normal—my dark hair, messed just so. I'm wearing my favorite blue jeans and dark-gray sweater. There's a comforting hum of people chatting. Everything *seems* normal, yet I still feel uneasy. *Focus, Sam.* I'm aware of being in the dream. It is an odd sensation.

I look out at the rain-swept street. I suddenly realize where I am as bright-yellow New York cabs stream by outside. *I went on vacation to New York once; I saw the Empire State Building.*

I shift in my seat and peer hard through the throng of traffic and pedestrians. Something doesn't feel right.

"I have to go," the man across the table says, looking at his watch. He's Indian, late twenties, appears a little nervous and on edge. "They'll know I'm here."

I turn to face him, only now aware of his presence. "But we just got here . . ." I begin.

"*You* just got here."

"I mean . . ."

"Sam, it's not my fault you were late," he says, standing and pulling on his coat. "Besides, you've got what you came for—and you didn't even have to break into the museum to get it."

"What?" I am confused. "But you didn't give me anything."

"You got what you came for," he says again. His eyes settle on a napkin on the table, which is covering an object the size of an apple. "Sam, be careful out there—this will get harder and harder, each of the thirteen steps, but it will be worth the journey. Don't let the bad dreams get you down. Oh, and Lora? Maybe next time you should make sure you're not followed."

With that, he's gone.

I turn to Lora. She's wearing a green shirt. I know for sure now that she's a friendly.

"Don't worry about Shiva, he's just spooked to meet you in person," she says, and I watch as she looks around, scrutinizing the scene outside the window. "He chose this meeting, this place."

"Well, we *were* late." I check my watch—as I look at it, the second hand stops.

Irritated, I shake my wrist as if that will help. The battery must be dead. "Shiva said we were followed."

We look around, first at the faces in the room, then outside.

"Over there!" I whisper, not pointing, trying hard not to give away that I've noticed the guy. "Across the street."

"Which one?" Lora says.

"The tall guy, gray suit. He's looking right at us," I say.

"Gray suit?"

"Yes."

"Are you sure?" she quizzes.

I nod.

"I can't see him." She peers hard out the window.

"He just walked behind a truck. He's an Enterprise Agent, isn't he?"

"How do you know that?" It's not that she doesn't believe me, it's more like she's testing me.

"Well, it's . . . it's like déjà vu. Like I've been here and seen this before."

"Can you remember what happens next?"

"Yeah, I'm working on it."

"OK, I see him. He's coming right at us." Lora then speaks rapid-fire into her phone, calling in help, as another Agent stops in the middle of the busy road, right next to the first. They're dressed the same, as if in some kind of uniform: gray suit, white shirt and a thin black tie. And they're just standing in the middle of the street, watching us.

I'm still staring as a truck drives right through them. "What the . . ?" I spill my coffee as I jump up in shock.

"Are they . . ?" Lora has turned her head away, can't bring herself to look.

The truck is gone, down the road. It didn't stop, in fact it didn't even slow down, not even giving a hint of hitting the brakes.

The men in the suits are still there, still *standing*, in the rain. In the middle of the road. Watching us.

"That's . . ." Lora pauses.

"Impossible," I finish.

The men start walking towards us—a taxi driver sees them this time. He hits the brakes but still swerves too late and smashes into a storefront. There is broken glass and screaming as the scene turns chaotic. But the men are still walking towards us. The taxi ran right through them as though they were made of air—and they're still coming our way. *What is happening? Is this what they mean by anything can happen in a . . . in a dream?*

The cafe around us has gone silent in shock.

"We have to leave!" Lora says, grabbing my arm. "Come on! Run!"

As the diners in the cafe jolt back to life and rush to the glass storefront to see the commotion outside, we rush towards the back exit.

Almost there, I remember. *The napkin on the table!* I race back, scoop it up and feel the object underneath—a round, heavy ball. The napkin opens and I see it's a dark crystal sphere.

"That must be what we came for," she replies. "Quick, let's move—they're almost here!"

I take a good look at the object—really concentrate on it. I try to hold on to the image of the most beautiful crystal I've ever seen. I can just make out that it's inset with a star-shaped pattern of yellow that glimmers brilliantly in the light.

I put the crystal in my pocket and we race through the busy kitchen and out the back door, into a wet alley. There are overflowing garbage cans and trash blows around in the storm. There are streets at either end with cars flashing by. Either direction, it's a fair run in the open—those guys are going to see which way we go. My heart pounding in my ears, we run to the right and towards the crossroad. I turn to check our tail.

They're on to us already! The first guy in the suit is close behind, along with four others, gray-suited carbon copies, chasing us down.

At the intersection with the main street I skid to a stop.

"Why are we stop—" Lora cuts herself off after bumping into me.

I look up. Between towering skyscrapers, the rain clouds are gone and the sky is blue and clear, the sun warm on my face.

"I just wished that it wasn't raining, and . . . did I do that?" I say.

"Yes, we're in your dream, Sam—you can control parts of it."

"Parts?" I hear the pattering of footfalls as our pursuers near.

"The more you concentrate, the more you can—"

The breeze shifts and we turn as one, as though feeling the same dread.

Around us, all the pedestrians and drivers are frozen in time. Every single person, even those guys in gray suits, is *completely* still. There's not a single sound.

"That's not me," I say.

"I know."

Lora and I look at each other in the silence—

And then an enormous *BANG* shatters the eerie quiet. It echoes down the street towards us.

I can do this. This is my dream, my destiny. Control it . . .

I slowly turn to face what I fear to see. The figure, Solaris, is there. The full-body black suit, the mask, like a giant robotic ninja who shimmers with a heat haze.

"I click my fingers," the figure says, "and—"

"Yes, I know," I say, my voice as steady and loud as I can muster, "and everyone around us dies, right? Unless I give you this crystal." I hold the glistening object out towards Solaris, who seems unfazed by my change of script.

"Yes." The blurred figure seems to shimmer at a higher frequency. "Give it to me or everyone *burns*."

Black-clad hands mime clicking fingers and I start. I ignore the flashes of memory from my past and of what is to come and try to focus on the moment.

Why am I here, again? To get information that could help us.

"Good, you're scared. *Feel it*. Now, hand the crystal over, boy." Solaris steps closer. "Pass it to me and you will be spared."

"You'll burn them all anyway," I say, my voice steady and calm. "You have no respect for life, this place, none of it."

"Never much liked this city," Solaris says. "But blame yourself—*you* brought us here."

I hold the crystal tight in my fist.

"No. This isn't where it happens," I say. "Not like this. This is only the beginning."

"Come now, Sam," he says, his harsh voice a goading whisper. "Here, there, beginning, end, it's all the same. You *know* what I can *do*."

"Yeah, well, I don't believe everything I dream."

"You're learning, but they only tell you what you want to hear, that they can make it safe for you in here. That going back will be the same as being there before. But it's not. It never is. I will haunt you at every turn, don't you see . . . you should start making your own decisions. You might be worthy then."

"Worthy? Of what? Crushing you?" I am fierce, angry, and can think of nothing more satisfying than punching Solaris in his shimmering black mask.

"Oh, ho. Is that what you think?" Solaris says, his grating voice somehow giving the impression he is excited. "It's so much more than that. I can't see the others lasting, but you—you may be different. I'm telling you, it will be the first Dreamer who's still there at the end. And I'd like you to be there at the end. We all need a competitor worth defeating."

"Like we all need a villain?" I say.

"Makes us *stronger*," Solaris retorts.

"For the race? It's a competition, after all, isn't it?" I say.

"Depends on how you look at it," he replies. "That presumes that there's a real opponent. The choice is yours—give the crystal to me, or I take it from your charred corpse."

"You'll kill us all anyway. But you haven't, and I think I know why—you still need me."

"There are fates worse than death," Solaris rasps.

"That's why I can't let you win." I stand firm.

"This is only our first encounter—as you say, just the beginning. You think I don't know that? This is my world, boy. Mine."

I shift on the spot. "Yeah, well, too bad I don't like to lose."

"This is no game. Now, give it to me!"

I can tell Solaris is on the edge, his temper frayed by my resistance. It is probably futile, but I can't help it. This is my dream, not his, and I want nothing more than to control it, to fight him and protect all the innocent people going about their business.

I pause. *Time to change things.*

"Sam, don't!" Lora yells.

I hold the crystal sphere in my outstretched hand, in a tenuous grip, as if it may fall at any second.

"No!" Solaris takes a stride towards me. "Don't be a fool!"

"I'll destroy it, if you don't—"

He moves again and I toss the crystal up into the air.

The scratchy figure of Solaris dives forward, reaching out for it.

I lunge right, taking Lora off her feet in a tackle.

"Close your eyes!" I yell as we hit the ground.

I land on top of her, a protective blanket.

"Let's see what I can do." The sky grows dark, thunder rumbles and rain begins to fall heavily. In a second, it's torrential, like a monsoon, the gutters flood and the street fills with water. *Yes*, I think, *that's it . . .*

Solaris grasps the crystal just before it hits the ground. As he does, he raises his other hand—and clicks his fingers.

I am too late.

Fire radiates out. *NO!* I scream in my mind, but it happens again, and despite all the water around us, I watch as everything glows and explodes—even Lora, who disintegrates in a flash of ash and we are all of us, gone.

Sam blinked awake. He was lathered in sweat, and his hands were gripping the armrests tightly. *Wow*, he thought, catching his breath, *that was amazing.*

"Sam, are you OK under there?" Jedi tapped the top of the helmet.

Sam nodded. "Can I take this thing off now?" he said.

"I've got it." Jedi unhooked the helmet and Sam stood up, stretching.

"Well, that was something," Lora smiled at Sam. She was already unhooked and was pouring cups of tea from an urn. "Well done. You were a natural in there, Sam."

"Like I've been dreaming my whole life?"

"Exactly!" Jedi laughed.

"I'm way tired now," Sam said, taking a cup of steaming tea. "Thanks. Were we under for long?"

"About four hours," Jedi replied. Seeing the surprise on Sam's face, he continued, "It can take a while, you don't notice it while you're asleep, usually. That said, sometimes it works the other way, where you could be under for twenty minutes and your dream takes you through years of events."

"Professor, what did you make of my dream? Did you see Solaris?" Sam turned to the older man, who was sitting in an armchair, looking thoughtful. Sam hoped desperately that all the answers were in the dream, that his work here was done, and he could go home . . . *well, wherever home is from now on*. He pushed aside the welling sadness about his parents and focused on the Professor's response.

"Unfortunately we can't see him clearly, but there is definitely a dark shadowy figure on the screen. Don't worry—it was still very valuable, Sam, thank you for doing that." The Professor looked at Sam and grinned. He seemed genuinely pleased. "I must analyze all that I have just seen and discuss our next step with the Dreamer Council."

"Cool," Sam yawned, as he held his comfortingly warm tea. "I can't believe I'm so tired when I've been asleep for so long."

"That's normal," said Jedi. "It's partly because of what we've done, forcing you into a dream state. But also, the intensity of the dream itself can take it out of you. You'll be all right after a good night's sleep."

"Why don't you go and relax, Sam?" Lora suggested. "We can pick this up again in the morning, can't we, Professor?"

"Yes, yes," the Professor agreed, but Sam could tell he was lost in his thoughts as he stood by the big screen where the images of the dream had projected for him and Jedi to see. It was paused on the moment when Sam tossed the crystal up into the air.

"OK, catch you later," Sam said. He was soon out of the lab corridor and taking the stairs up towards the dorms, unable to shake the implications of the nightmare he'd now seen in more detail.

Across the room, Alex was on his back, oblivious, snoring. It took Sam a moment to realize where he was.

The sun shone brightly through a gap in the curtain. There were faint sounds coming from outside the door. The other students were coming and going from their rooms. He was at the Academy. He had expected to wake up in his own bedroom, to the morning sounds of his family's daily breakfast routine. He felt like he'd relived the nightmare and needed to follow his routine of filling in the dream journal, take his five-minute shower, eat his breakfast and go to school. *Wow*, he thought. *I guess I won't be seeing my family for a while. That's if they're even . . . I'm not even sure I want to see them again, after a lifetime of lies.* He sighed in frustration. The nightmare was more real than ever, and he had a feeling that the Professor was going to tell him that he had to go to New York and face the monster, Solaris.

Immediately, his heart rate climbed and a sweat broke out down his neck.

He sat up on the edge of the bed, gasping for breath.

Alex woke with a start—"Sam? You OK?"

Sam was sucking in air, heaving in short, sharp breaths. His chest felt tight, a great weight on it.

Alex rushed over and seeing that Sam was in serious trouble, he ran out of the room, shouting for help.

"Asthma attack," the nurse said. "Sam tells me he's had some mild symptoms before. I suspect the excitement of the last couple of days brought on this extreme reaction." She frowned at Lora. "But he should be fine now, so long as he's careful."

Sam had a clear plastic respirator over his mouth and nose. The oxygen was cool and plentiful, and he felt both alert and drowsy at the same time.

"You all right?" Lora asked.

Sam gave the OK sign to his gathered companions. The nurse left his room, leaving behind a couple of inhalers.

"What happened, Sam?" Eva asked, her eyes filled with concern.

"I, ah, kind of . . . panicked I guess. I was thinking about the nightmare, and the flames and Solaris."

"Look, Sam," Eva said. "I think you need to tell us the truth."

"What do you mean?" he asked.

"You know," Alex said. "You owe us, if we're going to be

in this with you. We need to know what we're up against. What's the deal with you and fire?"

Sam looked at his tightly balled fists and forced himself to relax them. "I'm sick, can't this wait?"

"The nurse said you're OK. Spill," Alex commanded.

"All right." Sam reluctantly took a breath and told them his terrible secret. "It was about a year ago. My best friend, Bill, invited me over to watch movies and spend the night. We were super excited because his dad had just gotten hold of some fireworks and we were going to try them out. Well, on the night, his dad didn't let us have them and Bill got mad, so we took one into his bedroom to set it off out the window. We waited until about midnight, we'd watched a few movies by then and eaten our weight in chocolate and chips, so we were pretty keyed-up."

Sam paused as he remembered the awful night. They'd lit it together . . . it was forbidden, tantalizingly dangerous and yet seemed harmless. Except they lost control. Of course looking back, they never really had control, never had a plan of where the firework would shoot off to. The white-hot sparks ignited the curtains and the bedspread, and it seemed to take only seconds for the whole room to go up in flames. Sam hadn't been able to save his friend back then. He'd never let anything like that happen again.

"Well, anyway, we did it, and it ended badly. Bill was . . . he was killed. His parents and I escaped with burns. He died, and I lived."

The room was silent as they absorbed this news. Lora seemed the least disturbed, but Sam figured she'd been expecting the story. *I bet they all knew*, he thought. *All the Academy people. Typical.*

"What does that mean?" Eva asked, looking at Lora. "Does it change anything about the nightmare?"

"Maybe," said Lora. "It could mean that the part where fire burns the whole city is really Sam's traumatized mind creating the worst possible scenario that he can imagine. We can't rely on that part of the dream being true, that's for sure."

Sam was relieved. That had been the worst bit. "But hang on, does that mean that we actually don't have any idea how it is supposed to end because my damaged brain can't see the real ending?"

"Well, that's a bit harsh, Sam—you're not damaged. But yes, it means up to the cafe we're fairly sure events will occur that way, but anything closer to the fire happening is unclear." Lora seemed deep in thought.

Sam started to cough and he wheezed until he calmed himself and got his breathing back under control. *Relax . . .*

"I don't think he should be going anywhere for a while," Eva said to Lora, and Alex seemed to agree too.

"I'm afraid we may not have a choice," Lora said, looking concerned. "Based on the info we gathered from Sam's dream, and intel from our sources, it's going to happen very soon."

"What's going to happen?" Sam said.

"This race, New York, your dream . . . it's all happening much sooner than expected."

It was after lunch by the time Sam felt well enough to leave his room. He found the others in a small lounge by a window overlooking a craggy ravine.

"He's the only one who can do this?"

"Yes."

"Why?"

"Because it's his destiny, and we know what happens if we try to change too much . . ."

"Hey, guys," Sam said, announcing himself.

The Professor and Lora were there, along with Tobias, Eva and Alex.

"So, you can see into the future?" Sam asked the Professor.

"Not exactly, but in a sense, yes," the Professor said, "as Eva did, and as you have done."

"Then why all the worry around here?" Sam said, sitting on the arm of a plush couch. "I mean, with Solaris and the Enterprise or whoever, all these guys who are after us—if you're so good at this stuff, so powerful, why can't you track them, know where they are and how they'll act, so that we can avoid any future danger and attacks?"

"Because there are powerful Dreamers out there who have the means to remain unseen," Lora said.

"Even from *our* dreams," the Professor replied.

"Like Solaris?"

"Especially Solaris," the Professor said. "That's another reason why you and the rest of the last 13 are so important. *You* can see him clearly. No one else can. Until you came along, he was as good as a myth, a ghost."

That kind of made sense to Sam—how Lora hadn't seen Solaris in his dream.

"Sam," the Professor continued, "we played back your dream from yesterday. That object you couldn't remember before? We've identified it as a rare crystal, a sapphire actually, known as the Star of Egypt."

Details of it flashed up onto the screen of Lora's tablet.

"It is thought to be a sacred object, rediscovered only recently among a lost collection of Egyptian artifacts."

"What's so special about it?" Sam asked, not wanting to look too closely at the object from his nightmare.

"We don't yet know," Lora admitted. "We need to get it and study it to find out its meaning. I'm afraid we will have to go to New York tomorrow night."

"But that's too soon!" Eva said.

"That's when the crystal is going on display, and it's our best chance to acquire it before someone else," Lora said.

"What about Solaris?" Sam asked.

The Star of Egypt

HOME
MENU
CONTENT
HELP
SEARCH

The **Star of Egypt** is an ancient Egyptian sapphire artifact, believed to have been commissioned around the time of 1200 BC. It was rumored to be in the possession of Ramses II. The Star of Egypt has

THE STAR OF EGYPT—
SACRED EGYPTIAN SAPPHIRE

been purported in ancient myths to hold the key to great power. Leonardo da Vinci, who was obsessed with crystal spheres, is understood to have been particularly intrigued by these legends, however no evidence has ever been uncovered to support the claims.

Recent news

The Star of Egypt has been discovered! Click **here** for more information.

"We do need to be careful of Solaris," the Professor said. "He is dangerous. He has no sentiment, no feelings for anything other than power, so the stories go."

"But he's not a magician," Lora said, "and he's no walking weapon of mass destruction. We don't believe he can create a fire that would burn all of New York."

"What Lora is saying, Sam, is that it is imperative for the coming battle that you don't let the fear in the dream overtake you in the real world."

"Fine," Sam said, doing his best to appear resolute and confident. "When do we leave?"

The Professor smiled. "As soon as I hear that you're ready."

The nurse had given Sam the all clear. Next up—physical training.

"So, what exactly are we doing in this class?" Alex asked. Eva shrugged.

They stood alone in a small room off the gym. There were several padded mats on the floor.

"You will be learning some basic jujitsu moves," Lora said, entering the room. "And Sam could do with some practice before tomorrow. Sam, care to give us an intro?"

"Ah, sure," he said. "Either of you done martial arts before?"

Eva and Alex both shook their heads.

"Right," Sam said, "well . . . jujitsu is a Japanese martial art, and a method of close combat for defeating an armed, and perhaps armored, opponent, in which you use no weapon."

"Nice," Alex said, raising his fists. "I'm ready, let's rumble."

Sam laughed. "Lora, care to help me demonstrate?"

"Sure," Lora said, standing opposite him on a mat.

"'Jujitsu' means 'gentle technique,' so it focuses on manipulating your opponent's force against them rather than confronting it with your own force."

Sam nodded and Lora moved towards him. He used her momentum to flip her over his leg and onto her back, all the while holding her arm.

"As you can see," Sam said, "I am holding her pinned to the floor in a shoulder, elbow and wrist joint-lock."

Sam let her go and Lora got to her feet, nodding at Sam with respect for the skill he'd just shown.

"So," Lora said. "Sam and I will take the two of you through some basic moves, so that you will at least be prepared to disarm an opponent, and to get them to comply with your commands."

"Sweet," Eva said.

"Ah, yeah," Alex said, moving around on the spot as he squared up against Sam. "I can feel it, I'm gonna bring the heat . . . you ready to meet Dr. Flash and Mr. Hulk?"

"What?" Sam said. "Those are your fist names?"

"You know it," Alex said, clowning around. "But be warned, I'm about to enter expert mode."

"Bring it," Sam replied, standing side-on and ready. "Try touching my nose. You do, and I'll make your bed for the rest of the week."

"Fine," Alex said, ducking and weaving, Sam mirroring his movements to keep a distance between them. Alex lunged—and Sam flipped him.

"OK, you won round one," Alex said, out of breath and flat on his back. "Best out of three?"

Sam helped him to his feet.

"Remember," Lora said as she practiced with Eva, "you want to use your attacker's energy against them, rather than directly opposing it."

"I think I've got it," Eva said, trying out a move that Lora showed her, but failing because she was holding back.

"Don't be afraid," Lora said. "Do as I showed you. Try again."

Sam and Alex did the same, and after half an hour Alex gave in and told Sam that he'd be his butler for the next fortnight.

"OK," Alex said to him, panting. "You're the Kung Fu Master."

"Jujitsu."

"Yeah, whatever," he said, hands on his knees to catch his breath. "Now, please, teach me how to do some of those cool moves."

"Who's that girl?" Sam asked Pi. They were having dinner in the hall. Sam was happy that he could feel lost in these moments before he had to leave and face his nightmare.

"Where?" Pi said.

Sam pointed to a blond girl who was reading a novel and blowing bubble gum.

"The one blowing bubbles?" Pi said, noticing the look on Sam's face. "No, don't get interested in her."

"Why not?"

"Everyone knows she's desperate to be part of the prophecy," he said. "I heard this morning that some students here expect to get their dreams in the coming weeks—they want to be part of the last 13."

"But who is she?" Alex asked, joining in the conversation with a plate full of chicken and rice.

"Violet," Pi said. "She never goes anywhere without her posse. Her best friend is that girl next to her—Pepper."

Alex said, "I think they're cute."

"Look at you guys," Eva said.

"What?" said Sam.

"Checking out the girls."

"Boys will be boys," Alex said.

"Yeah," Eva said, "well, you don't stand a chance with them."

"Really?"

"Really. Has any girl ever talked to you of her own free will?" Eva said. "No, I didn't think so."

"You know," Alex said through a mouthful of food. "I've often wondered why that is."

"Got a mirror?" Eva replied as she got up and walked towards the exit.

"Ooh! Zing! You got me!" Alex called to her back, mock hurt on his face.

"You know, Eva is kind of pretty too," Pi said.

"Oh, you think so?" Sam said.

"Oh, gross!" Alex said. "To me she's like the big annoying sister I never had."

"She's younger than you," Sam said.

"Really?"

"By a few months, I think," Sam said. "And you're nearly a year older than me."

"Humph."

"Well," Pi said, watching as Eva left the room, "I think she's wonderful."

ora and Tobias joined them at a recreation area below the main dorms

"I still don't get who this Enterprise is," Eva said, "or who they represent."

"In short," Lora said, "it started out as a way of trying to better *scientifically* understand the power of dreams."

Sam asked, "Why's that so bad?"

"Times were different back when they started," Tobias said. "They wanted to find out the secrets of accessing the dream world for the government, to use as weapons."

"They wanted to weaponize dreams?"

Tobias nodded.

"And what do they want now?"

"We're not exactly sure," Lora said, facing a big window looking out at the mountains. "These days they're a private outfit, and they still study Dreamers, like we're lab rats or something. And they're forever looking for the last 13 and related clues—they've got archaeological teams all over the planet, people placed in universities—they're everywhere."

"I've heard they've become friendlier," Tobias added.

"I've heard otherwise," Lora replied.

"What's their connection to us?" Sam asked.

Tobias looked at Lora accusingly. "You haven't told them?"

Lora shook her head.

Tobias' eyes softened when he looked at Sam, and then the others.

"They created you," he said.

"What, were we born in one of their labs or something?" Alex asked, but his joking expression turned serious when he realized that Tobias meant exactly that.

"They've long been experimenting with DNA," Tobias explained. "You're likely to be especially gifted with your dreams because they used DNA from the most powerful Dreamers of previous generations."

"And this was to somehow make weapons out of us?" Sam asked.

"My guess is that these days they'd use your predictive abilities for more economic gains," Tobias offered.

"Huh?" Alex said.

"Imagine going to a company and saying that you've accessed their competitor's plans," Tobias explained. "That you've seen all their secrets. That you can replicate their products. Or even better, beat them to producing their next big moneymaker."

"We're just lab rats . . ." Eva said, staring absently.

"Lab monkeys, more like," Alex joked.

"It's not funny!" she said to him.

"Come on, Alex!" Sam snapped. "You can't pretend like you don't care all the time."

"Yeah, well, we're a science experiment and our parents are not our real parents," Alex said. "So don't you both get all soppy now. Do I care? Maybe. But who's to say I'm a lab freak like you two?"

Alex stormed off. Eva had tears in her eyes.

"It's OK," Sam said to her.

She nodded, wiping her runny nose.

It was going to be a long, sleepless night for them all.

The next morning, storm clouds blotted the stained-glass windows in the main hall. Sam, Alex and Eva had been asked to go and see the Professor. Sam had butterflies in his stomach that reminded him of so many nervous events—his school's debate finals, his jujitsu gradings, soccer tryouts. The other students seemed silent, giving them space.

As they walked into the Professor's office, they heard: "Professor, I can't protect him from—"

Lora abruptly stopped talking. Tobias was there too, and he went over and welcomed the three of them.

Sam sat and noticed that they were all watching him. *Do they expect me to talk, or maybe they are just getting a final look before Solaris turns me and a million others to toast?*

"I'm ready," Sam said.

"What if he doesn't go?" Eva asked, cutting Sam off. "Then maybe—maybe this guy can't get the Star on his own. Maybe no one will die."

"Yeah," Alex added, "if Sam's not there to hand it to him, then the bad guy doesn't get it, right?"

"He'd find a way," Tobias said. "Our best hope is to control the scenario as much as we can, and avoid loss of life. Besides, much worse things may happen if the dream is changed too much."

"Maybe not," Eva countered.

"There can't be any 'maybes' with this," Sam said. He looked at Alex and Eva and he could see that they had accepted it. He knew that they'd put up that show of a fight to somehow put him at ease. He appreciated it more than they'd ever know. He looked at the Professor.

"But we'll be with you," Tobias added. "Lora, Sebastian and these two." He motioned to Eva and Alex.

"But—"

"No *buts*," Eva said, cutting off Sam's objection. "We're in this together. If you're going out there, taking action, then so are we."

"It could be your best chance to alter what happens," Lora said approvingly. "Changing the parameters here and there puts you on a slightly different path. It alters what we've seen in the dream. It all helps."

Sam looked from the Professor to Tobias, then the others in the room. "You sure you guys want to do this?"

"It's our destiny to guide you, Sam," Tobias said. "But you're the one actually going into the arena."

"Like a gladiator," Alex said. "Cool."

"Yeah, but one with friends!" Sam checked Alex and

Eva's reaction; they smiled. *Friends it is, then.* "OK, we started this together, let's finish this together."

"We leave in five!" Lora said as she ran out of the entry hall, crunching across the snow-encrusted gravel to the waiting jet.

The Professor began to say his goodbyes. Tobias, Alex and Eva walked over to the plane.

"You're not coming?" Sam asked the Professor.

"I have work to do with the Council. We have to devise a global plan if we're going to have any chance of defeating Solaris."

"But how can I have a hope of winning against him?"

"You'll be fine, Sam. You'll be in good hands," the Professor said. "We need you to come back safely, as some on the Council suspect that you may hold the key to finding the remainder of the last 13."

"But . . . I'm just an ordinary kid," Sam said.

"With some extraordinary dreams," the Professor replied, chuckling. "No one's ordinary. Look at your friends there, willingly going to face danger with you."

Sam felt guilty because of that.

"What if this is a case of mistaken identity?" Sam said, looking for a last chance to back out. "An accidental dream I had, which only resembles the start of this race, but it isn't really?"

The Professor again laughed quietly. "Sorry, Sam, this isn't like the movies."

"What?"

The Professor smiled. "I mean, you're not the wrong person in the wrong place at the wrong time."

"But we're just a bunch of teenagers."

"That's how it's supposed to be," the Professor said. "When the time comes, you'll be ready. Think of what happens if you turn your back on this—evil will rise up and reign supreme. World wars, pandemics, worldwide tragedies . . . everything people have ever dreaded will become reality."

"Sounds a bit far-fetched . . ."

"I'm afraid it's already begun," the Professor said. "Solaris already wields great power and searches for more, with no thought to the loss of life or effect on the earth. Here, take a look at this."

The Professor handed Sam a newspaper article. The headline read:

TREASURE HUNTERS HUNTED. TEN DEAD.

In recent days, a group of treasure-seekers have rampaged just outside Cairo, causing widespread landslides, implosions and sand erosion at key archaeological dig sites.

An unspecified number of Berlin University-backed dig workers are missing and ten were killed when their underground tunnel system was caved in by unauthorized earthworks in the area. It is believed that a group of illegal dig workers are responsible.

It is rumored that a group of treasure hunters are in the area searching for a particular treasure, which may or may not still be there. It is unclear how they are achieving this devastation, but one possibility is that they are working mainly at night.

Grave fears are held for sanctioned dig workers, and dig operators are being warned to keep their people out of the area until this savage group can be found and detained.

There have also been unverified reports of sink holes, taking carloads of people into the ground, on dirt roads close by the dig sites. The land and environment minister has concerns over the integrity of crucial arterial roads leading into and out of Cairo, and is pleading with truck drivers, motorists and train drivers to keep a watchful eye on the roads and report any sinkages immediately. He says, "These lunatics must be stopped. The very livelihood of our great city is at threat. Mark my words, we must find them before our supply routes are cut off, or I fear there will be terrible consequences."

"Sounds like a nightmare." Sam was shocked. "You think Solaris is responsible for this?"

"Yes, we believe he is searching for ancient relics of power, clearly with no thought for the lives of the people in the dig sites, not even for the whole population of Cairo. But this is just the beginning. If Solaris was to ultimately prevail, it would be a nightmare in waking life for seven billion people. It's our job to stop that from happening."

"What about this stuff in Cairo? Who is going to stop that?" Sam asked.

"We must leave that to others. The 13 have the nightmares. It is their sacrifice in this war, and sadly, possibly not their only one. Other people have their own jobs to do. Trust me. If you focus on Solaris, and live out your nightmares, the rest will follow."

"I just want to be like everybody else," Sam said.

The Professor put his hand on Sam's shoulder.

"But you're not, Sam. We're not. We all have to accept our destinies."

As he turned to leave, the Professor leaned in to Sam, "You've foreseen what happens in New York—remember it, use that advantage, and change it."

Sam strapped into his seat on the supersonic jet. Eva was opposite, facing him, and Alex slouched in the seat across the aisle. There was a group of Guardians in the back playing poker and keeping to themselves. Sam was ruffled, but he thought carefully about the conversation he'd just had with the Professor and knew he had to tell them something.

"Right, so apparently not only am I the one who has to save us from the forces of evil," Sam said to them, "but I might also be some kind of walking, talking Rosetta Stone—the key to finding all of the last 13."

"Wow, so it's a starring role for you, then," Eva said.

"I know, right?" Sam looked out the window. *Is Eva annoyed?* Sam wondered. *I really don't get girls sometimes.*

Lora sat down opposite Alex. "When will we know if we're part of the last 13?" Alex mumbled.

"I don't know, Alex. But regardless, you all need to believe you can do this, get through this battle," Lora said. "Believing is the biggest part. The rest will fall into place."

"You make it sound easy," Sam grumbled.

"I believe you can do this, even if you don't believe it

yet," Eva said. "Just trust that the right thing will happen. I did, back on that helicopter, and look at what happened."

"What if the right thing is that I can't do this? If I'm meant to fail?" Sam said. *So, she's not annoyed, then. What about Alex?* Sam looked across and saw Alex surreptitiously picking his nose and humming distractedly. *He's OK.* But Sam couldn't stop worrying about what the Professor had said. There was more at stake than just their lives, more than one city even. The whole world was in trouble. *It's too much for this small group to take on, surely.*

Lora looked at him for a long moment and then said with a gentle smile, "You can do anything you put your mind to, Sam—you'll see."

Flying fast over Europe, they chased the sun west. Sebastian was piloting the aircraft and Tobias was in the main cabin, talking with Lora, making plans.

Sam, Eva and Alex sat together, trying hard to show each other how relaxed they were. The three of them were dressed in Stealth Suits, which currently looked like cool civilian clothes. The suits were made from some sort of secret material the Academy had "borrowed" from the military and fashioned into clothing. Jedi had explained them as bulletproof jumpsuits, and in their regular appearance, they looked like the bodysuits race-car drivers wore. The fabric could physically change shape and style at the direction of the wearer. The stealth aspect was their ability to change appearance by refracting light and projecting a holograph of how the user wanted the suit to appear. Sam's suit now resembled blue jeans and a charcoal-colored sweater, just as he'd seen in his dream.

"What about an extra vest or something?" Alex said. "Like, you know, to be super bulletproof."

"You won't need it," Tobias said. "At any rate, the

Enterprise won't be shooting at the three of you, you're potentially priceless. Besides, the Enterprise might be our adversaries, but they're not monsters. We have never deliberately hurt one another. Well, aside from a dart here and there."

"So that explains the dart guns," Eva said. "That's a bit of a relief, actually."

"But who knows what might happen now that the race has started for real," Lora added. "And remember, they're not the only ones we have to worry about. Someone was prepared to shoot down your helicopter . . ."

"Anyway," Tobias said, "these suits repel all darts, stabbing weapons, and most shrapnel from blasts."

"Most?" Alex said.

"Well, let's just say that if you sit on a bomb, don't expect to be walking straight the next day," Tobias said.

"Right, don't sit on a bomb, got it," Alex said.

There was awkward laughter, followed by an even more awkward silence.

"Well, here's something I don't get," Eva volunteered. "Why don't Dreamers use their dreams for good—like through their premonitions they could foresee accidents, or natural disasters, and save lives?"

Lora looked pained. "A few years ago, I went through many arguments with the Professor about that sort of thing, as many Dreamers have argued before."

"And?"

"I was told that humanity had to follow its own course," she said. "That if you intervene with things like that, it dramatically alters too much of the future; the more we change things, the less predictable the future then becomes in subsequent dreams. We may think we'd be helping but, in truth, we might leave the future open to something much worse."

"Like what?" Sam said.

"Things that we'd never see coming."

Sam stared out the frosted plane window. The skyline of Manhattan was spread out below. The brilliant orange glow of the low sun glinted off the tall glass towers. Below them, millions of lives were busy being lived in these streets, oblivious to the destruction that could be about to unfold.

"Buckle up for landing," Sebastian announced.

Sam could see the lights of JFK Airport as they banked— then they flashed by it, flew south over the East River, took a tight sweeping curve around the harbor, passed the Statue of Liberty and turned up the Hudson River towards Manhattan's West Side.

"Um, where are we landing, exactly?" Sam asked.

"The *Intrepid*," Lora replied.

"Where?"

Lora looked out her window. "There." She pointed.

They all looked out their windows as they came in through a large arc over New Jersey, headed for—*the city?*

"That's the river, and the city," Alex said. "I don't see any runway."

"It's the *USS Intrepid*," Lora explained. "It's an aircraft carrier."

"But," Sam objected, "that ship is a museum!"

"And it's closed for maintenance right now, so it's a good landing spot for us," Lora said.

"But people will see us!"

"This aircraft has stealth technology," she said. "Just like your Stealth Suits, but on a grander scale. Besides, we don't have time to waste. Just be ready to get out and move clear of the aircraft quickly because Seb will take her back up and wait for our call if we need a quick evacuation from Manhattan."

They came in fast, the jet slowing only at the last moment and then hovering into a vertical landing. Sam's stomach still dropped from the sensation. No sooner had they touched down, than their belts were unbuckled and Tobias had the exit door open. They piled out onto the deck of the *USS Intrepid*, the Guardians forming a protective perimeter around them.

Sam looked back as they cleared the jet—it was nearly invisible, taking on the surrounding elements of the river and the parked aircraft. He saw Seb waving at Lora and then—*WHOOSH!* The aircraft was up in the air, warm exhaust from the engines washing over them, and it flew away to the south, quickly becoming invisible to the eye.

"Come on!" Lora said, leading the way towards the pier, as the group ran after her.

"Tobias, Eva and Alex will head to our safe house," Lora said, directing who would go where. "You stay put and be ready to move in and give the Enterprise a distraction if needed. There is a group of Guardians already waiting there for you."

"Are you sure we've got to split up?" Eva asked.

"I'm very sure," Sam said, not wanting to put his friends in harm's way. "Lora and I have to go alone to get the Star of Egypt—only this time, we'll have Guardians undercover outside."

"Why not change it more?" Eva said. "Change the way it happened in your dream?"

"We already are," Lora said. "We're changing the little things. But we'll still use our contact to get the Star for us and it's safer for all of us if only two of us meet him."

"Who is he?" Sam asked.

"The man from your dream."

"He's Enterprise," Sam said and he saw the acknowledgement on Lora's face. "But . . . he also works for the Academy?"

"Yes, in a sense," Lora said. "And, most importantly for us, he's somehow got access to the Museum of Natural History."

"What's our plan?" Sam asked as the group of them jogged to the road to flag down a couple of taxis.

Tobias and Lora looked at Sam. "It's your dream, which means you set it up," Tobias said.

"What?" Sam said, thinking about it. "You're saying *only* the Dreamer can alter their dream?"

"It's the best way. You're in the driver's seat," Lora said. "You've seen things we haven't—it's your intuition we need. Trust your gut. What would you change?"

Sam thought about it. "How about we change where we meet our contact?"

"I like it," Tobias said. "It's bold, but we just might get away with it."

"Where?" Lora asked.

"The museum," Sam replied. "Instead of the cafe, let's meet him at the museum."

Sam looked back at Eva and Alex. Eva had dreamed how they'd met, how they were loaded aboard a helicopter that had been shot down. *She did nothing to change that, and it all worked out OK in the end, didn't it? Maybe I got my dream wrong? And Alex . . . well, we don't even know why he got picked up. Has he even had any true dreams yet?*

"It's OK, Sam," Lora said, signaling for the group to slow as they neared the street. "The right thoughts will come at the right time . . . don't force it, just let it come to you. When it feels right, you'll know how it's meant to be."

Tobias stood by the open cab door.

"I'll be close by," he said, "and Seb has been briefed on

the change and now has the bird hovering over that part of town, so we're both ready to move in and help out if you need us."

"I still think we should stick together," Eva said.

"Yeah, c'mon, we're jujitsu masters, we can help!" Alex said.

"No, guys, they're right," Sam said. "Only Lora and I should go to the meeting."

Eva looked dumbfounded and Alex looked annoyed.

"This is really it, isn't it?" Eva said.

"I guess so, yeah. See you on the other side." The nerves settled in Sam's stomach but his head was spinning as he saw a flash of his nightmare.

"You've foreseen what happens . . . use that advantage, and change it." The Professor's last words to him rang in his ears as he worked to change the future, just enough.

"OK," Sam said, "let's do this."

Lora and Tobias shook hands, then she was in the cab, waiting. The Guardians were already on their way, having taken the first cab they'd flagged.

"Be careful," Eva said to Sam.

Sam nodded.

"Don't go saving the world without me," Alex said. "The gang's gotta get involved in this stuff too, you know."

"Yeah."

"I'm serious, I can take this Solaris punk."

"Next time, Alex." The false bravado made Sam grin.

Sam got in the taxi next to Lora.

"Sam," Tobias said, ducking his head into the back of the cab. "Trust your instincts. When the time comes, you'll know what to do."

Seeing that familiar face so full of confidence filled Sam with the genuine belief that he could change what he'd dreamed, that he could somehow defeat this Solaris creature.

"Thanks. See you soon." Sam smiled nervously.

Tobias looked at Lora. "Contact me or Sebastian if you need help," he said.

The door closed and the taxi merged into traffic. Sam, however, was in no great rush to meet his destiny.

Lora closed her phone. "He's going to meet us at the cafe but earlier," she said.

"Not the museum?"

"He can't. Seb's been scanning radio channels and has noticed a whole bunch of Enterprise activity in the area around the museum—there's too much heat there."

"Well, so much for that change, then," Sam sighed. He hesitated, then said, "Look, Lora, I've been wanting to ask . . . this guy, Shiva . . . how is it that he's helping us?"

"His father pioneered computer systems for NASA, while being there at the beginnings of the Enterprise," Lora replied. "And Shiva's said to be just as smart. He's highly regarded around the world as a hacker and programmer. We—and this was before my time—secretly orchestrated that his father change allegiances, and Shiva followed in his father's footsteps there too. He's been our insider at the Enterprise ever since."

"So he works at the Enterprise while giving you guys inside information from them?"

Lora nodded.

"Is that how you found out about us? Did he leak the phone calls to you?" Sam said in a burst of curiosity. "Do you have other contacts there as well?"

"Yes, yes, and I can't say. It's on a 'need to know' basis," Lora replied coolly. It looked as though the Academy were not above keeping secrets themselves. "It's for your own protection."

Sam considered this information and resisted the temptation to get annoyed about it. *Not now*, he thought.

The cafe was just as Sam had remembered from his dream. The tablecloths, the sounds, even the people all seemed right.

"Weird, isn't it?" Lora said as they sat at a table.

"It's totally like déjà vu again," Sam said. "It's like I've been here, lived this experience, but I know I was only here in my dream."

"You were here," she said, "and now here you are—it's the one event seen over and over."

"Only I get to change things now. This all makes my head hurt." Sam looked out the window. "I hope we can make things different."

"We already have," Lora said. "We're here early . . . earlier than Shiva."

Sam thought about it and smiled.

"That's true," he said. "We were late before."

"What else do you notice that's different?"

"Well, he said we'd been followed," Sam said. He looked out the window, but he couldn't see anything untoward, certainly no Enterprise Agents. Their two Guardians stood outside, big guys in suits—that was different. Another pair waited in a car. Sebastian was flying above the city somewhere. Tobias and Sam's friends—with another squad of Guardians—were at the safe house, ready to bring in the cavalry. "I guess we weren't followed this time. I hope."

The waiter brought them water and they ordered drinks. Sam ordered a hot chocolate.

"Really?" Lora said.

Sam laughed. "Just changing the little things where I can."

"What is it?" Lora asked, noticing that Sam was looking at her shirt.

"It was a different shirt you were wearing."

"You said green. This is my favorite green."

"Well, I'm just saying, in my dream it was . . . darker?"

The shirt, part of the Stealth Suit, changed hues on cue.

"Better?" she said.

"On second thought, maybe change it back?" Sam said, as Lora started to look a little exasperated. "Sorry, we're changing the little things, remember?"

Sam looked around to see if anyone had noticed and smiled as the waiter delivered their drinks and some bread.

"Aren't you afraid that someone might have seen that?"

Lora sipped her espresso. "Sam, I'm more afraid of what they're going to see in the next thirty minutes."

"**S**orry I'm late," Shiva said, taking a seat across from them. "I had to shake a tail."

Sam's panic rose as images of his dream flashed in his mind. And the fact that Shiva was followed this time.

"But I thought you . . ." Sam trailed off. Why would he be followed—unless his fellow Enterprise Agents suspected him? Or was it someone else?

"Sam . . ." Shiva said, staring at Sam, a look that was full of wonder. "It's good to meet you."

"Shiva, did you bring it?" Lora interjected.

Shiva put a small box on the table. Sam couldn't quite believe the crystal was actually in there . . . that this dreamed-of moment had arrived.

"This is really happening, isn't it?" Shiva said, as if echoing Sam's thoughts. "The search for the last 13 has begun."

Lora nodded. She took a deep breath and gently opened the box. The crystal was just as Sam had dreamed it.

Shiva said, "And Sam is . . ."

"Yes," Lora replied. "He's started it all."

Shiva looked at Sam with what could have almost been pity.

"Good luck," he said to him. He made to leave.

"You're going?" Sam asked.

"I have to get back."

"Wait," Lora said, sitting still. "Don't both look at once, but across the street, there are two Enterprise Agents by the newspaper stand."

Sam looked from Lora to across the street—two guys were dressed for the part of Enterprise Agents, in the gray suits, white shirts and black ties. This *was* playing out to match his dream. Instead of repeating and continuing his dream, he said to Lora, "But we were careful."

Shiva replied, "You were followed."

Lora looked a little spooked.

"But we made sure! Maybe you didn't shake that tail after all," Sam said. "Why wouldn't they trust their own employee, I wonder?"

Shiva looked uncomfortable. "I have no idea," he said coolly.

"Well, regardless," Lora said, "those guys in the suits out there prove someone was followed. We should get out of here."

They all stood up and as they did so, Sam looked across the street again and then back at the box. There was something about the crystal . . . *no, it's not right . . .*

"This isn't it!" he said, looking at Shiva. "This isn't the Star of Egypt!"

34

everal things happened at once.

Lora's phone rang—Tobias.

The Agents moved towards them, crossing the street, drawing weapons as they neared.

The Guardians outside raced to intercept the Agents.

The car containing the other two Guardians exploded in a huge fireball.

Sam stood frozen, his mouth agape. Lora sprang into action and dragged Sam away from the table . . . just as Shiva turned to reveal the grenade in his right hand—and then he pulled the pin.

BANG!

The explosion was a loud pop and then an incessant hissing as Sam coughed in a thick plume of choking orange smoke.

"Smoke grenade!" Lora said loudly into Sam's ear. "Keep low and run, out the back!"

Shiva had disappeared.

Sam was transfixed at the sight of the Enterprise Agents outside, coming for them. One was running and firing his pistol at the Guardians, who'd taken cover behind a parked yellow taxi, while another stood there staring back at Sam. The gray suit, standing in the rain. He was in the middle of the road and started walking towards them. *Just like my dream . . .* but then a taxi beeped and swerved to avoid the guy, running into a flower store on the other side of the street with a *SMASH!*

"Move!" Lora pushed Sam forward, heading to the kitchen. He could make out that she was on her phone, talking to Tobias at the safe house, calling in help.

"What?" She paused behind the counter to listen carefully to her phone and Sam bumped in close. "OK."

She looked at Sam.

"You were right, Shiva never got the Star of Egypt," Lora said to Sam. "It's still at the museum. Tobias and the others are on their way there now!"

The smoke soon filled the whole cafe; diners screamed and coughed. Gunfire pattered out front, Guardians and Agents locked in battle.

"Come on, this way!" Sam said, as they finally made it through the kitchen, hot steam and the clanging of pots and pans all around them. They burst out from the maze of doors and receiving bays to the alley at the back. Sam stopped and considered another familiar scene.

Lora was back on her phone. "Sebastian, we need a pickup! We're in the alley behind the cafe!" she yelled urgently.

Sam remained paused in their getaway, the alley empty so far.

"Which way?" Lora asked.

He looked left and right, the coast seemed clear . . . in his dream they'd gone right, and though he didn't want to make the same choices, he was starting to wonder if changing these little things really made any difference.

"Sam!" Lora implored. "Which way? Think back to your dream."

"No," Sam said, a stillness overcoming his nerves. He began to feel certain. "It's different this time. This way!"

He led off to the left. Lora was running full pelt, updating Sebastian on the direction they were headed. They were already halfway down the alley.

"Coming in hot, ten seconds!" Sebastian's voice came over Lora's speakerphone.

This is already different from the dream, Sam thought. *Maybe we've done it!*

A vehicle came screeching around the corner, turning into the alley. A huge blacked-out SUV drove straight at them and blocked off their route ahead. Sam could make out the driver's gray uniform—*Enterprise*.

They turned and ran back the way they had come. Just as they neared the back of the cafe, an Agent appeared from the bay doors.

Lora drew her dart pistol.

The Agent aimed his.

Sam sidestepped up the ramp, twisting through a jujitsu fly-kick that connected with the Agent's gun arm, sending his aim off as—

WHACK!

Lora's dart drilled the Agent square in the neck.

Sam and Lora didn't hesitate, they continued to run.

"We have to make it to the street!" Sam yelled.

The noise behind them was growing louder—the vehicle roared up the alley and an Agent emerged through the sunroof, aiming a huge launcher at them.

"Get ready to—" Lora yelled.

Above them was the deafening whine of the jet engines as Sebastian brought the aircraft into a hover just above the tops of the buildings. A hatch opened underneath and a rope ladder dropped down some fifty yards ahead of them.

BANG!

Sam, still running, turned to see—

"Whoa!" he twisted his body to avoid a huge net that barely missed him, tangling up a couple of steel trash cans instead. It would have wrapped him up tight, like a big game safari prize.

He ran faster to catch up with Lora, the ladder nearly within reach as Sebastian feathered the controls of the aircraft above.

The SUV was still hammering after them, the engine noise growing nearer and nearer.

Sam shot a quick glance behind them. The car behind roared past the rear of the cafe, with reckless disregard for the Agent still out cold from Lora's dart.

The gunner standing out of the sunroof had changed— now there was a female Agent bringing up another bigger, weapon.

"Lora!" Sam yelled and in the same instant he grabbed the back of Lora's shirt and pulled her into an alcove at the back door of a store.

WHOOSH!

The hot vapor trail blasted by them as the rocket flashed along the alley.

They looked around the corner from their cover—the rocket streaked straight up into the sky.

"It's heat seeking!" Lora yelled into her phone. "Sebastian, look out!"

They watched the jet bank suddenly, away from the alley, in an attempt to avoid the blast.

But it was too late.

The rocket hit hard just behind the cockpit of the Academy aircraft, the explosion engulfing the whole fuselage as the flaming jet slipped from view.

A long second later . . .

BOOM!

All the windows along the alley shattered, showers of glass raining down as the force of the aircraft's explosion blasted the streets below.

"Come ON!" Lora yelled, kicking down the door behind them.

Sam's mind was reeling, but there was little time to think. He stayed close behind as they sped through the back of a store, running through racks of clothes, startled shoppers and yelling staff telling everyone to get out fast. Out in front, heavy rain was falling on the street and thunder clapped loudly. They headed in what they guessed was the direction of the crash site, bumping through the crowd which was a sea of black umbrellas.

This is the rain that fell in my dream . . . and that wasn't thunder.

The people around them were screaming and fleeing as the aircraft crash set off secondary explosions, the blast having ruptured some gas lines, sending large chunks of hot debris through the air.

Across the street and three blocks down, the wreckage of what was left of the aircraft was strewn over the ground. Several vehicles and a building front were ablaze. With chaos reigning, Sam and Lora were nearly alone on the sidewalk as pedestrians sought safety in large buildings and subway stations. Sam looked towards the crashed jet and felt a sickened shiver run through him.

"Sam!" Lora said. "We have to go!"

"But Sebastian—" Sam couldn't believe Lora would just leave the scene like this.

"He's gone!" Lora said, her voice cracking slightly. "There's no time to lose. We have to go, we have to get to the museum!"

They were passing the front of some glass-fronted stores at a full run when Sam tripped.

As Lora doubled around, reaching to help him up, they caught the reflection in the store's windows . . . a dozen Enterprise Agents were behind them, converging, fast.

"Run!" Lora said—but they were out of time.

The big black vehicle from the alley pulled up with a

squeal of rubber on the road. A woman got out. She was Sam's height, with big square shoulders that made her look like a wrecking ball. It was the Agent he'd seen fire the missile at the Academy jet.

Now she had a gun in her hand, leveled at the pair of them.

"Don't try anything," she said. "I won't miss this close."

Sam and Lora stood stock-still.

"Try to stay with me," Lora whispered out of the corner of her mouth. "But if we get separated, the museum is about ten blocks north. I'll meet you there."

Then, Lora called out to the woman, "Let us be on our way!"

The Agent laughed as her cronies closed in on Lora and Sam. A few pedestrians raced by, oblivious to this show-down. Sirens announced the pending arrival of emergency crews to the crash site.

"I know who you are, Lora," she said. "And there's nothing you can do to stop us. We're here for the boy. You can walk away."

"Just leave now!" Lora commanded.

"Or *what?*" the Agent said, looking around, feigning fear. "You'll give me nightmares?"

Lora was about to answer when somebody fired.

The Guardians, from the backup crew at the safe house, had come out of nowhere, their armored car pulling up in a cloud of smoke between them and the Agents.

Lora pulled Sam inside the back door as bullets and darts ricocheted off the vehicle.

"Go!" Lora yelled to the driver, who already had his foot planted. He knocked cars out of their way as though they were speeding in a tank. "Get us to the Museum of Natural History!"

Sam peeked over the backseat to see the Agents now over a block behind in the chase. He looked across to see Lora watching too, the reflection of the jet-wreckage flames burning in her eyes.

Red carpet ran down the massive set of stone stairs at the front of the building. Spotlights strobed and sliced through the rain-filled air. A gala event was about to begin.

"It's like these people didn't even hear that explosion," Sam said, bewildered.

"Manhattan's a big, noisy place," Lora replied. "If something doesn't happen right on your street, you might never know about it."

Throngs of people milled around. Cameras flashed as limos came and went.

"How will we get in?"

Lora looked at him and without a word spoken, their Stealth Suits changed—they were both now wearing police uniforms.

"Really?" Sam said.

"It's an access-all-areas pass," Lora explained as she got out of the vehicle. "Come on, follow me."

"Lora, wait." Sam tried to explain. He was too young to get away with looking like a cop. But Lora wasn't in a listening mood. He followed her out of the car, and read the exhibition sign—

ANCIENT EGYPTIAN SECRETS REVEALED!

Tonight, the unveiling of the newly discovered cache of Egyptian antiquities. Be the first to see this treasure, lost since the 16th century.

"Sam?"

Sam recognized the voice and his blood chilled. He was busted. He turned around.

"Hi, Xavier." It was Xavier Dark, the rich, smart, popular kid from school.

Xavier looked him up and down.

"You got pulled out of class the other day, loaded aboard a military helicopter, and now you're a New York *cop*?" Xavier asked incredulously.

Sam looked at his uniform, then up at the dashing figure of Xavier in his expensive black-tie getup.

"He's working on a special undercover operation," Lora said to Xavier. "It's a national security matter, so keep your lips sealed, young man."

Sam smiled at the phrase *national security*, as he was sure that Xavier would have heard it being shouted out in the classroom by the Enterprise Agent.

"So you are . . ." Xavier said, impressed. "What are you involved in here?"

"Can't say," Sam said. "Sorry, national security and all that. How about you?"

Xavier motioned to the big banner hanging above the museum's entrance.

EXHIBITION SPONSORED BY
THE DARK FOUNDATION

"My family paid for the expedition as well," Xavier said. "You want to come and say hi to my father?"

"Maybe later," Sam said, thinking that he really *didn't* need to see his psychiatrist right now—there'd be a whole lot of explaining and analyzing to do. "We've gotta get moving. Later, Xav."

"Right," Xavier said. Sam and Lora were already walking away, headed inside, when Xavier called out, "Sam—there won't be any trouble tonight, will there?"

Sam smiled and called over his shoulder, "Nothing a bit of money can't fix!"

Inside the museum, Sam followed Lora as she wove through the guests to a cloakroom.

"Ah!" Sam jumped a little when he saw his suit change to a black-tie tuxedo. Sam had never worn a tux before and he liked it. Lora, who was now in a slim black dress, took a glass of champagne from a passing waiter.

"Just fitting in," she said. She looked around the room and Sam watched her—her eyelashes were wet.

"I'm so sorry about Sebastian." Sam felt terrible. What else could he say?

"We'll have time for that later." Lora's lip trembled, but she held it together. "Right. Well, let's do this, then."

Sam followed her through the crowd to the exhibition hall, where he took a program listing the night's festivities.

"Let's head upstairs," Lora said. "We'll get a better view from the balcony."

"'The largest cache of Egyptian antiquities to be revealed to the world this century,'" Sam read from the pamphlet as they walked. "It says here that they are going to do a live opening of the largest crate."

"That could be it." Lora pointed down to the lower level, where the crowd was gathered around a large wooden crate upon a raised platform. "That might hold our Star of Egypt."

"No—look!"

Lora followed Sam's pointing finger. There, on a black pedestal behind a red velvet rope, was the crystal from Sam's dream.

"I can't believe it's right there in the open like that! How do we get it?" he wondered.

"I'm not sure yet," she said. "I'll check in on where Tobias and the others are."

As Lora spoke on her phone, Sam looked at the faces around them. Several he knew from seeing them on television. There were people from the uptown parts of New York, with a smattering of sports and entertainment figures among them. He checked his watch—it'd stopped working. He tried his phone—it was dead. He turned to Lora, who was taking her phone from her ear.

"They, um, they got held up but they're on their way," she said.

"Lora," Sam interrupted, looking around the room and noticing that while most of the people were lost in chatter, there were a few who were tapping their watches and checking their phones. "Does your phone work?"

"Of course," she replied, holding it up to show him. "I just made a call . . ."

Her voice trailed off when she saw the screen was now blank, and she looked up at him, surprised. Then all the lights in the room went out.

37

People screamed, but immediately the emergency lighting flickered on. Flaming torches around the exhibition hall were lit by attendants. The orange light of the flames danced in the faces of those assembled and Sam could see them smiling and cheering—it was all part of the show.

"And now!" Dr. Dark said through a microphone, standing by the side of the crate with the mayor of New York next to him. "We reveal what has been hidden from archaeologists for so long!"

"My phone," Lora said, looking again at the blank screen, "all the electronic devices have shut down."

"But the lights?" Sam was uncertain.

"Emergency only."

"What could do that?"

"Some kind of jamming device . . ." Lora was looking around.

"The Enterprise?" Sam wondered, getting more nervous by the second.

"Just stay close," she said.

Sam felt his Stealth Suit change and saw Lora's morph too—into the kind of tough-looking, combat bodysuit he'd first seen her in.

"And now, I give you . . ." Dr. Dark motioned for a few guys to come forward as they held on to shiny crowbars that were inserted into the corners of the crate.

"That can't be right," Lora said as they leaned over the railing and she recognized some faces below. "Why are these Guardians here?"

Lora's expression turned from curiosity to alarm as a dozen Guardians moved in towards Dr. Dark.

"Could it be the long-lost . . ." Dr. Dark began as the sides and lid of the crate were removed. There was a gasp of amazement from the crowd. "Yes! It's the long-lost half of Ramses the Great's tablet—the famous Dream Stele!"

Cries of wonder and loud applause rang out, which quickly turned to murmurs of discontent as many of the guests realized that their cameras and their phones were not working.

"Sam," Lora whispered, "the top half of the Dream Stele of Ramses II is the ancient tablet the Professor mentioned at the Academy. It shows an ancient version of the prophecy about Solaris. But we've never had the whole story."

"Because the Stele was broken?" Sam remembered the conversation at the Academy, clear as day.

"Exactly, it was broken in two. Whole, it could reveal

everything we need to know to win the battle!" Lora was excited.

"And Dr. Dark found it . . ." Sam surmised.

"And with it, the missing half of the prophecy," Lora said urgently. "We have to get down there."

There was rapid movement as the Guardians muscled through the crowd, converging at the raised dais from all angles.

"Are those Guardians going to get the Dream Stele for us?" Sam asked.

Lora shook her head, confused. Then she stopped and stared up. Sam noticed it too—there was smoke pouring out of the air vents all around the room. It was orange, and it smelled just like the smoke grenade used by Shiva back at the cafe.

"Sam," Lora said, kneeling fast, "get down!"

As if in slow motion, Sam saw two Guardians throw smoke grenades into the middle of the crowd.

BANG!

At the same moment as the grenades went off, the smoke was so thick in the air upstairs that the sprinkler system was activated. There was a maddening rush as people clamored for the exits amidst the gushing water.

"I can't see!" Sam said.

"Keep down until it clears," Lora replied. They huddled close to the ground, peering through the handrail, catching small glimpses of the mayhem below.

They spotted Dr. Dark, trying to keep everyone calm.

The Guardians were still near the Stele—in fact, a couple were up close to it.

"Lora, what are they doing?"

Before she could answer, the Guardians turned and fled the scene. Sam and Lora instinctively dived back as the air roared.

KA—BOOM!

The force of the explosion sent flying debris smashing everywhere, throwing Sam and Lora across the wet mezzanine floor.

"Let's move!" Lora hissed, and they struggled to their feet.

The scene below was one of utter destruction.

Where the newly rediscovered half of the Dream Stele had been, there was now a gaping hole down to the basement level. Sparks lit up the smoky darkness as the remaining museum patrons spilled out of the emergency exits.

The Guardians were nowhere to be seen.

"Wait!" Sam called. He put a hand on Lora's arm to stop her from heading for the stairs.

There, entering the room below from the main doors, a group of firemen changed before their eyes—their uniforms replaced with gray suits. At the front of the pack was the woman who'd fired the rocket, killing Sebastian.

"So the Enterprise has Stealth Suits too?" Sam said.

"Any technology we have, they have," she replied. "Only better."

"Great," Sam whispered. "What now?"

"We have to get the Star of Egypt."

Sam scanned the ground level, and saw that the case containing the Star had tipped over in the blast. The floor was covered in clumps of stone that had been the Dream Stele. There were pieces of broken concrete and tiles from the floor, all covered in water pouring from sprinklers that continued to gush. The Enterprise Agents were sifting through the debris, clearly looking for the crystal sphere. *Great, just great . . .*

"Why would the Guardians have done that?" Sam whispered.

"I don't know," Lora replied, keeping low to the floor and watching the Agents closely.

"Come on," Sam said to her.

"Where to?" Lora asked.

Sam pointed to the fire escape behind them.

Downstairs, peering through a gap in the door, Sam could see that the group had split into two search parties. There were three Agents in each, at opposite ends of the expansive room, looking for the Star of Egypt.

"What now?" Lora asked from behind him.

The lights in the room flickered for a moment, then finally all flashed out in a shower of sparks as they shorted from the sprinkler water. In that moment, Lora's phone rang—the sound echoing around the fire escape stairwell.

"Answer it!" Sam said, as he hastily closed the door. The ringing was sure to attract attention.

"I'm trying!" Lora said, her wet hands fumbling.

The sound of quickening footsteps got louder.

"Move! Go down!"

Sam pushed Lora ahead of him, down to the next level on the fire stairs as the door behind him flew open and Enterprise Agents entered, hot on their heels.

Lora turned at the landing, her dart gun drawn and fired upward—

PFFT! PFFT!

Darts plunged into each of the two lead Agents and they slumped forward, tumbling down to the landing.

Sam followed Lora as they sprinted down another level. She spoke into her phone as they ran, descending yet more stairs and entering the sub-basement level of the museum.

Sam jammed the door shut behind them. "Hopefully that will hold them off for a while."

"Tobias is in a car chase leading a group of Enterprise Agents out of the city," Lora said, reloading her dart gun. "Their Guardians turned on them. Tobias had to take them out."

Sam balked, but didn't have much time to think

about how his science teacher may have "taken out" those hulking Guardians.

"Eva?"

"They got separated, but she's headed here," Lora said. "We'll worry about them later. Right now we need to find a way up to street level."

"What about Alex?" Sam persisted.

"They'd decided to split up earlier. Tobias must have sensed something was wrong," Lora said, then looked around them warily. "He took off and we don't know where he went. Hopefully he will keep out of the way and not try to be a hero."

A banging at the fire door behind them made Sam jump.

"We have to get that crystal!" he said.

"Pick your battles, Sam," Lora said. "We've lost this one. Come on."

"But—" Sam was desperate, *we are so close!* He couldn't just let the chance go by.

"No! We're done here!" Lora was adamant.

Sam followed after her as she ran down a corridor, to a huge room that opened up into a cavernous warehouse space for larger exhibit items. Water pooled on the floor from the gaping hole above.

"Sam, come on!"

"Wait," he said, running over to the hole that had also been blown through this floor, though no wider than a manhole in diameter.

"Sam!"

He looked up while Lora crouched nearby, her weapon drawn, as four black ropes dropped down and the Agents, led by the woman, began abseiling down through the larger hole above them.

PFFT! PFFT! PFFT!

There was a cry as one Agent let go of the rope and fell to the ground in front of Sam with a sickening *THUD*, two darts in his leg.

As Sam reached for the Agent's weapon, the sound of darts flying back and forth, echoing in an exchange of fire between Lora and the descending Agents, he saw it through the hole . . . the Star of Egypt glistened in the emergency lighting, resting only a few feet away on the level below.

"Sam!"

He turned to see Lora get hit by a dart and she fell backwards and out of view behind a large carved-stone monument. In the same moment, he saw what she was warning him of—

Two Agents had been hit, dangling in the air unconscious, tethered by their ropes. As if in slow motion he saw a cylindrical metal object falling towards the floor.

A grenade—different this time, not a smoke grenade. He'd seen enough movies and played enough computer games to know that this was the kind that went *BOOM!*

He dived for the hole in the floor and saw a flash of gray as an Agent bumped into him. As he twisted down the hole, legs first, he watched helplessly as the grenade fell towards him.

Sam opened his eyes. He couldn't hear anything for a moment and then suddenly his ears were ringing to the tune of giant bells. In his hand was the Star of Egypt.

He was on his back on a hard tiled floor having miraculously survived the explosion. Sam thanked his jujitsu training for his fast reflexes. He felt surprisingly OK . . . it didn't feel like anything was broken. *Maybe the Stealth Suit broke my fall?* He could just make out a sign to the left of his head: 79th Street.

I must be down at the subway level now.

It was deserted, dark. The only light came from a couple of flashing neon tubes and sparks from the hole in the ceiling above.

He tried to get up but realized something heavy was on top on him, pinning him down.

A figure.

It moved.

An Agent?

It had a black outline, it wobbled and blurred, seeming a little groggy.

Sam rolled it off him and got to his feet. Too fast—his vision blurred and he found it hard to focus in the dim light.

No.

No!

It can't be true!

The fuzzy, blurred outline, the black bodysuit, the full-face mask.

Solaris.

Sam scrambled away, desperately searching for a weapon, searching for something, anything.

Solaris slowly straightened to his full height.

"Sam, Sam, Sam . . ." It was *that* voice, loud even above the ringing in his ears. It cut right into Sam's skull.

They stood there, facing each other, barely any space between them.

Sam looked across at the escalator that rose up beside him. *I could try to outrun him . . .*

"Give me the Star, boy!"

Sam turned back to face Solaris—his nightmare come true. Sam remembered the burning cars, buildings, people . . . *and the real devastation that has begun in Egypt . . . and Sebastian. So many lives already lost.*

No, no running.

"No," Sam said.

Solaris tilted his head.

"You want this?" Sam held the Star of Egypt in his hand

so that Solaris could get a look at the glinting surface. "Come and get it."

He put the Star on a bench next to him.

And so Sam stood there, waiting, ready, hoping he could live up to his destiny. *This can't be really happening . . . but it is.*

"You're a fool," Solaris said, taking a couple of weary paces forward.

"And you're not as big as you were in my dream," Sam said.

"You will be sorry for this." Solaris neared. He side-stepped to the left and Sam mirrored his move, wary, watching.

The breeze shifted and carried with it the sound of a train approaching.

Solaris moved first, a charging strike, which Sam easily parried.

The rumble became deafening and the express train flashed through the station.

For a moment, the two figures' moves were highlighted by the strobing lights of the graffiti-covered carriages.

Sam waited in a jujitsu stance for the next attack to come. *Control your breathing: one, two, three . . .*

Solaris' arm came swinging at him, but Sam shifted his weight and carried the momentum through a roll. They both sprang back to their feet as one.

"I see you've had some training," Solaris said, pacing

side to side, Sam following suit to keep a useful distance between them. "It won't do you much good."

"If this is all you've got," Sam countered, "I think I'll do OK."

Solaris nodded. Pounced.

Sam blocked the kick—but the follow-up punch to his head was too quick in the dim light to counter and he was knocked to the ground. His head reeled from the blow, but he twisted his legs and got up in a split second. *Ignore the pain, stay focused.*

The Star of Egypt was on the bench behind him. *Better keep it that way.*

Solaris came at him again. Sam went on the offensive, kicked out—it was blocked. Solaris' fists were flying at furious speed now, each blow countered, but Sam ceding territory as a kick sent him slamming back against a steel column.

Stunned, the pain coursing through his body, he fought for breath—but there was no time.

Solaris punched at his throat. Sam ducked.

CLANG!

Solaris backed up a few paces, clutching his hand.

Sensing an advantage, Sam sent a high fly-kick at the masked figure's cheek that whizzed through the air, missing as Solaris backed away too fast. But Sam was at him again—flipping through his kick and closing the gap and punching, attacking with an unrelenting pace, fists pounding at Solaris like jackhammers.

Solaris grabbed hold of a wayward arm and twisted Sam around, pulling him into a choke hold.

Down the tunnel, a train's headlights burned two holes in the darkness.

"We have rules . . ." Solaris whispered in Sam's ear, "about not killing your kind . . ."

Sam was choking. His fingers fought at the tight hold around his neck.

"Which is why I've turned my back on my own," Solaris said. "Some things can only be done a certain way."

Sam's eyes watered and his face felt like it was going to explode.

"This is where you die, Sam . . ."

James Phelan started writing his first novel while in high school. He now divides his time between writing thrillers and books for teens. **jamesphelan.com.au**